Indigo
Dark Republic Book Two

D.L. Young

For My Godfather, Mike Salerno

CHAPTER 1

I should have told this lightweight to go fuck himself an hour ago, should have left him there in the middle of nowhere.

"Fresh from the market," he boasts. "Picked it up over at Lake Livingston yesterday morning."

It's an absurd lie, and the urge to roll my eyes is a strong one, but I resist.

"You won't find nothing better 'round these parts, trust me."

Sorry, old man, but this woman's not in the trust business.

I take another swig of tequila from my flask, disappointed to find it's the last swallow, then I look down again at the stash of food the bone-skinny old wanderer called *an embarrassment of riches*.

He sees the doubt on my face and tries to reassure me. "Come on, now," he urges. "It tastes better than it looks, I promise. Have a little faith."

The midday sun blazes down and I wipe sweat from the back of my neck. An hour's drive out of my way for this: a half-empty barrel of rotten vegetables and a bag of mostly rancid meat.

One time out of a hundred, I tell myself. That's about how often someone wandering the wastelands will be sitting on a deal worth doing. This would be one of those other ninety-nine times.

And long odds aside, you should have known better anyway, Indigo. The more they talk, the less they have, and this crusty old crook's been chatting nonstop since we picked him up. I look at the old man and shake my head, my expression telling him he's wasted my time.

"Now I know them peppers might be a bit soft around the edges, but they're good eating," he insists, though now there's a clear backpedal in his tone. "Yes, ma'am, them's good eating."

He removes one from the barrel—a green bell pepper that's mostly black and nearly falling apart—and stuffs it into his mouth to try and prove his point.

The greenies quietly watch the goings-on from behind me, learning the finer points of…not very much, now that I think about it.

I peer down into the barrel one last time. Not all the peppers have gone bad. "Two liters of water for the lot," I tell the old wanderer.

He answers with a shrug and a creepy, toothless smile, then waves me over for a private conversation the greenies won't hear. Against my better judgment, I step toward him, moving my shirt to the side so he can see the pistol tucked into the front of my pants.

He leans in close. "I tell you what," he says, keeping his voice low as he glances behind me, "you can keep the water. How about you give me some alone time with one of them youngsters?"

Ah, humanity, you never disappoint. So this is what I drove an hour out of my way for: a fuck-freak selling the last food he probably has in the world for a piece of ass.

I stare at the man without blinking, letting a long moment stretch out until he nervously breaks eye contact and starts to fidget.

"How about this," I counter. "I take the food off your hands, and I don't tell anybody down in New Waverly where to find you. Sound like a fair trade?"

The man's face twists up in confusion. "What're you talking about?"

"We both know where you stole this food from: down at the market in New Waverly."

He looks crossly at me, lifts his chin, like I've just uttered the worst offense imaginable. "Ma'am, I did no such thing, and I don't care for the accusation."

Right. You'd trade rotten food for a quick lay, but you'd *never* steal peppers, would you? Christ, the indignation's almost comical.

"I bought all this at the Lake Livingston market," he protests, "just yesterday morning like I told you."

"Peppers, tomatoes, cornbread, eggs, tamales, you name it," I say. "I've bought anything and everything down at New Waverly since I was a kid. You think I'm not going to recognize Old Rita's peppers when I see them, even when they're half-spoiled?"

The wanderer's wrinkled face melts into something less certain, less confident.

I take another peek into the barrel. "On second thought, you might be right. Maybe these aren't Old Rita's peppers. Maybe when I tell them what I came across, she'll tell me it's my mistake, that nobody's stolen anything from her lately. Maybe she won't send her six sons out here to find you."

The man licks his lips and his eyes dart back and forth like some animal caught in a trap. I turn my back on him and walk away.

The greenies watch me, young eyes staring, waiting to see what happens next. "Shooter," I say, "take the food, toss it in the back of the truck."

"You got it," he answers, scrambling into action.

Enough of this. We've wasted enough time this morning. I trudge up the hill so I can get my bearings from the high ground and figure the quickest way out of here. The old wanderer follows close behind, pleading with me the whole way.

"Come on, ma'am," he begs, "you gonna tell me you ain't never lifted nothing in your life? And you can't just take it without giving me nothing for it."

I pull out my binoculars and keep climbing up the hill. "I'm giving you exactly what you paid for it."

We reach the hill's crest and I scan the countryside around us. To our immediate south is Huntsville, its sprawl of ancient, decaying, and mostly deserted homes and buildings nestled close to the old Interstate 45. What's left of the highway—concrete rubble and jagged steel rebar, most of it covered by undergrowth—weaves a crooked path through the thick canopy of pines and post oaks. The morning sun, already torturous and not even noon yet, fries the back of my neck. I adjust my shirt collar to cover the exposed skin, and then my neck and shoulders stiffen as I spot what the wanderer, so intent on his begging, hasn't yet noticed.

"Come on, now," he pleads. "You don't want to get a reputation as one of them traders who don't deal fair, do you? A reputation is all a trader—"

He suddenly shuts up, and that's when I know he's seen them: a row of what looks like old telephone poles about a quarter-mile away, cut off to maybe ten feet high.

And although they're too far away to make out clearly, we both know what the small round objects atop each of them are.

Human heads.

*   *   *

Heads on spikes. It's not the kind of thing you run across every day, not the kind of thing you expect to see around these parts at all, in fact. It takes the wanderer about five seconds to scramble down the hill and hop on a motorbike he's got hidden in the brush. He kick-starts the motor and takes off in the opposite direction, leaving a cloud of dirt and his embarrassment of riches behind.

A knot ties itself in my stomach, but I won't let myself panic. A panicky trader's a worthless trader.

All four of my crew run up the hill to see what's going on, to find out why the old man took off in such a hurry. They spot the poles and stare for a few moments, trying to work out what they're seeing.

Jak, a skinny kid with a peach fuzz mustache, lifts his hand to his forehead to block the glaring sun and squints. "What is it?"

I pass him my binoculars and he lifts them to his face. He gasps, then snaps the binoculars away from his eyes, hands them back to me. "It's heads on top of them poles," he sputters, then he hunches over and throws up.

I shake my head, watching all those calories come pouring out of him, money wasted feeding him breakfast. Then Pablo joins him. More of my money splatters onto the dirt. The other two stand there with their mouths hanging open, staring at the distant poles, each topped with the head of some poor sucker who wasn't able to cut a deal.

"Fundies?" Shooter asks. "Is it Fundies?"

That's what the old wanderer must have thought, no doubt, when he lit out of here. The Fundamentalist Church of Divine Wrath has a bent for these kinds of public statements. It's not uncommon to see bodies hanging from trees with signs reading HEATHEN around their necks if you wander a bit too close to Fundie-held turf down in the southeast. Call it a warning to nonbelievers, a gruesome border marker, whatever. I've seen plenty of neck swingers and heads on spikes in my time, but I've never seen a Fundie landmark this far north. Never this close to *my turf*.

I peer through the binoculars to get a better look. Skin dark and shiny like old leather, baking in the hot sun, grotesque expressions frozen in pain. The pole in the center has the word REPENT scrawled into the wood.

I scan the area for a couple minutes, find no sign of anyone. The knot in my stomach tightens. First the wanderer's crappy deal, now this. *Not a good way to start your morning, Indigo Cruz.*

Behind us there's more retching. Jesus, why did I even feed them in the first place? Better they empty their stomachs here than in my truck, I suppose.

"You're gonna pay me back for that breakfast," I call back to them without turning around.

They're greenies, I remind myself. Small towners, every one of them. And judging by their reaction, it's a safe guess they've never seen anything like this.

Well, get an eyeful, kids. If you end up becoming a trader in my turf—if this doesn't send you running back to whatever out-of-the-way, off-the-map shithole you fled from—it isn't the worst thing you'll see in the wastelands. Not by a long shot.

I take out a rag and wipe sweat from my forehead, pondering the poles, the heads, what they mean.

It's just about the last thing I would have expected, running across something like this on a route I've traveled countless times without incident. And if there's one thing twenty years of buying and selling in these wastelands has taught me, it's that the unexpected is almost always bad. Bad for trade, bad for me.

"We should go back, right, Miss Indigo?" Jak's chin is shiny with spit and barf, his eyes wide with fear. Miss Indigo, these greenies always call me. Like I'm a schoolteacher or something. I toss him my rag.

"Clean up your face."

"Yeah, we have to go back, right?" the girl whose name I keep forgetting pipes up. She nervously tucks a strand of hair behind her ear. "I mean, isn't this a warning or something?"

The others join in, peppering me with question after

question. Have I seen this before? Are we in danger? Is it really Fundies? Aren't Fundies supposed to be down near Houston?

Now I'm wishing they'd go back to throwing up.

"Quiet," I bark, and they fall silent.

So I guess this discovery will be their lesson of the day. They won't learn the finer points of trading natgas pellets for provisions down in New Waverly like I'd planned, but they'll take something else away, maybe something more important.

"This is what we call an unexpected event," I tell them, motioning toward the poles. "And on a trade run, something unexpected means risk. And risk is a trader's enemy. Risk is the thing that'll make you pay a premium for pellets, for water, for food. Risk is the thing that'll get you shot up by a gunbird. Risk is a tricky little son of a bitch that you don't want any part of. Two kinds of traders like risk: poor ones and dead ones."

They stand there, watching me, listening.

"It's risky enough just to wake up and make it through the day without getting your throat cut. Risk isn't something you ought to go looking for. Let somebody else play with risk. Some true-believing Fundie or some soldier in Guzmán's army. Let them die for risk. A good trader doesn't fuck with risk. A good trader, a competent trader, knows how to make money without ever stepping anywhere near that rattlesnake named risk."

I move my eyes over each one of them, letting the words sink in. No one speaks.

"All right," I announce, "let's get out of here."

We make our way back to the trucks we left parked in a copse of cottonwoods.

By the time we get there a few minutes later, my unlucky day has become unluckier. There's a group of Fundies with shotguns waiting for us.

*   *   *

The shocks of the old ambulance squeak like worn-out bedsprings as we rumble along the uneven ground. Two Fundies sit on the bench near the cab, watching over us, shotguns across their laps. The men are shoeless and dressed in threadbare UN refugee rags. They could be twins, both with the same shaved heads, same scrawny arms, same hateful stares. Maybe they are twins. The only difference between them is their tattoos. Their *holy markings*, as they'd call them. One has the creation myth covering his right arm. His shoulder displays a white-bearded god with arms raised, sun and planets and stars exploding from his hands, the images flowing down and terminating at the man's wrist. The other arm is Eden, a dense pattern of greenery interspersed with animals and the doomed couple standing there in fig leaf underwear. The other Fundie is pure Old Testament blood and gore. Battles and swords and spears cover his arms, shoulders, and neck. Holy warriors versus infidels. His forearm's a portrait of David holding up Goliath's severed head.

The ink work's shitty, artwork's worse. Wiggly outlines, uneven color. Self-drawn. Classic Fundie.

One of them notices me staring at his arms and I look away. They have our wrists tied behind our backs and our ankles bound. The five of us sit on the floor of the ambulance, quiet and blank-faced under the hostile stares of our minders. With each bump the ancient vehicle's thin, corroded steel flexes and bows under my rear. The ground blurs by beneath us, visible through a rusted-out patchwork of holes and tears. Next to me is Jak, his lower lip quivering under that not-quite-mustache. Across from us sits Pablo, staring at the floor with hopeless eyes like a prisoner who's just learned his sentence. The girl whose name I still can't recall is beside him, her forehead resting on her knees, her expression hidden. Beside her is Shooter.

We've been heading south at a plodding pace for about

an hour. My back muscles are bunched up tight and aching from the awkward position. I straighten up and twist my torso, trying to get some relief. Old Testament Fundie glares at me and racks the slide on his shotgun. *Cha-chak!* Pablo and the girl cower at the sound and Jak makes a yelping noise that reminds me of a small dog.

"You sit still," the Fundie with the Genesis tattoos growls.

The greenies are scared to death, probably about to piss themselves. All except Shooter. He's staring right back at the Fundies, scowling, almost daring them to blow his head off. I sigh and wonder how the kid ever made it to fifteen. He's got the wrong mix of balls and brains, Shooter. Too much of one, not enough of the other. I have my doubts he'll ever cut it as a trader. Security, possibly, but he'll have to learn to check that quick temper of his.

I give Shooter a stern look out of the tops of my eyes. "Go easy, boy. There's no play here." Last thing I need is a hotheaded kid mucking up this situation even worse than it is.

Jak whispers to me, his voice shaky and thin. "What are they going do with us?"

The other greenies turn their gazes my way, their faces twisted in anxiety, anticipating some kind of answer. They want to hear that they'll be okay, that their heads won't end up at the top of a pole.

I could tell them that we're not really in danger—at least not the kind they think we're in—and that to me this looks and feels like a shakedown, nothing more. And a shakedown isn't anything to worry about if you know what you're doing. It can even be an opportunity if you work it right. I could tell them that if these Fundies wanted us dead, they wouldn't have bothered to tie us up and pile us into this rust bucket. I could tell them this has happened to me a dozen times before, that more than a few of my turf negotiations and trade deals started out with my hands tied behind my back.

But I want them quiet, and they're quiet when they're scared, so I shrug and answer, "I don't know."

The girl turns her eyes downward, and I can almost feel the hope leak out of her.

Hope! That's her name. Finally.

We roll on. What are they doing here, these Fundies? They're too far north, too far from their home turf. Maybe they're not legit Fundies. Maybe they're just wannabes or some new offshoot. If we're lucky, they're starving to death, and from the looks of them they just might be. An empty belly is a rash, careless negotiator. An empty belly cuts the first deal that'll end its hunger. I love empty bellies. They're easy money, every time.

Pablo looks up at me, his eyes blurry with tears. "I'm scared, Miss Indigo."

Thanks, kid.

Never say my name in front of strangers. How many times have I told them? A dozen? More? Goddamn greenies, they're going to be the end of me. If I could run my turf without greenies and under-traders and runners, you bet your ass I would.

I stare knives at Pablo. He seems to realize his mistake and quickly lowers his brainless head in shame. Then I glance over at the Fundies, and oddly enough, they don't react to hearing my name.

Which most likely means they knew it already, that they were out looking for Indigo Cruz *specifically.*

Damn.

So now the stay-quiet-and-wait plan doesn't feel like the best play. I need to know what they know.

I look over at Old Testament. "How much longer to camp?"

He narrows his eyes at me, doesn't answer.

"I have to take a piss," I say, fidgeting back and forth a bit like I can't hold it back much longer.

"You just hold it," he grunts. "Camp ain't that far.

Won't be long now."

Genesis Fundie elbows him, as if to say he shouldn't have answered.

So now I know there's a Fundie camp not more than a couple hours' drive from my turf. Wonderful.

"How's the hunting around these parts?" I ask, probing further.

Old Testament leans forward, looks at me like I'm crazy. "The hunting? This is your turf, trader. You oughta know the hunting 'round here way better than us. We only got here a month ag—"

He's cut off by a second elbow to his ribs, this one harder. He looks sharply at his partner, annoyed.

Genesis glares at Old Testament the same way I did at Pablo moments earlier. "Not another word, you hear me?"

So they've been in the area a month. I ponder that for a moment. Could the Fundies have expanded this far north already? It doesn't seem likely. They've got Houston, everything around it, and a good portion of the Gulf Coast. Expanding northward—especially this far northward—doesn't make sense. There's nothing around here. No natgas fields, no major towns, nothing of value. If they were going to expand, taking a bigger stretch of the coast would be the smart move. More ports under their control means more sea trade, more money coming in. This far north, there's nothing worth taking.

And then it hits me. *Conroe.*

The refugee camp at Lake Conroe. Last I was down there was months ago, maybe a year. At the time there were a couple hundred of them, pitiful souls pitching tents and living on catfish, most of them driven from their homes and scared shitless by Flaco Guzmán's relentless land grab out west. I had more money in my pants pocket than the whole lot of them put together. Complete waste of time, that trade trip. Came back empty-handed, not even a barrel's worth of rotten vegetables to show for it.

Lately there's been a lot chatter on the trade channels

about Lake Conroe. Refugees pouring in by the hundreds, thousands. Rumors of a massive UN relief mission coming.

Up near the border with the States, where most of the refugee camps are, relief supplies get looted all the time. The UN drops off the fuel, supplies, and food, and the minute they leave some local militia rolls into camp and snatches it all up, leaving the poor bastards as hungry and buggered as they were before the relief convoy arrived. Fundies aren't above such things.

The more I turn it over in my head, the more it makes sense.

"Making a move on Conroe, is that the plan?" I ask bluntly, hoping to catch them off guard.

Genesis stares at me without blinking, trying to mask his reaction, trying not to give anything away. Old Testament's mouth slowly falls open, and he looks at me the way a child looks at a carnival magician who just made a bird disappear. He's clearly the dimwit of the pair, too dumb to hide what he's thinking. Under different circumstances, an excellent pick for a poker game.

Genesis glances at his partner. "Like I said, not a word," he mutters.

But it's too late. Old Testament's already given it away. God bless the idiots in this world. What would a trader woman do without them?

So that's it. Conroe. That's what they're after.

And that explains why they picked us up, why they looked for *me* in particular. They'll want to know the best way to get to Conroe from here, if there are any hostile towns on the way, and whether or not Dallas has any gunbirds routed nearby. And who better to give all this up than the woman who runs the biggest trade turf in the area?

By the time the ambulance comes to a stop some minutes later, the pieces feel like they've come together. Why they're here, what they want, where I fit in.

I scan the greenies' faces, forcing down a smile at their utter hopelessness. They've got so much to learn. This is a gift, what's happened here today, not a death sentence. Odds are we'll get a much better payout than a milk run to New Waverly.

The back doors swing open and daylight pours inside, blinding me for a few moments. Old Testament grabs my upper arm, yanks me to my feet. "Get on out."

Squinting, I step out of the van, feeling confident as my eyes adjust to the sudden brightness.

Overconfident, I suddenly realize.

Standing before me is Reverend Zachariah Wright. *The* Reverend Wright. It's unmistakably him, a large man with rosy cheeks and a wide gut, dressed in a white linen suit and matching wide-brimmed hat. The founder of the Fundie cult, one of the most powerful figures in the Republic. I stand there, staring. I'd expected to be dealing with a Fundie soldier, or maybe even a higher-up in Wright's church. But not the man himself.

He's grinning at me like he's just had a big meal and I'm dessert.

I swallow and attempt to compose myself, trying to fathom just how deep the water is that I've just been thrown into.

"Indigo Cruz," Wright announces, spreading his arms wide. "I am so pleased to make your acquaintance."

His greeting booms with what sounds like genuine joy, his eyes flash with what looks like sincere affection. It's the kind of welcoming smile you'd give a favorite cousin you haven't seen for years.

A smile that scares the hell out of me.

CHAPTER 2

"I hope your transportation wasn't too uncomfortable," Wright says.

I rub my raw, chafed wrists. "It was fine."

We walk through the Fundie camp, trailed by two bodyguards. Tents spread out all around us, dozens of them, scattered through a forest of towering pines. Under our feet fallen pine needles crunch with every step. We pass by a pair of young men—kids, really, maybe around twelve years old—sitting next to a small fire, cooking some kind of bird on spit. A scrawny pheasant or dove, looks like, barely a meal for either of them. One of them turns it slowly. They look up at us, notice the reverend, then scramble to their feet and bow their heads respectfully. Their clothes are threadbare rags.

Wright returns their nods. "Gentlemen." We walk on, the reverend setting the pace at a leisurely stroll.

The camp's eerily quiet. The few who mill about are all armed. Shotguns strapped to shoulders, holstered pistols, sheathed machetes. Nearly everyone sports clumsy tattoos on arms, necks, and faces. The telltales of Fundie soldiers. Crusaders, they like to call themselves. They eye me warily with piercing, hot stares.

Keep your head in the game, Indigo. Have to figure out the angle here. There's always an angle. You just have to find it.

A light drizzle starts to fall as we arrive at a large tent. Wright extends his arm, politely bobs his head. "After you."

I push through the door flap. The inside is a sudden shock of comfort and luxury. Hardwood floor, leather chairs, a large desk of thick oak with ornate carvings of cherubs blowing trumpets. A small air-conditioner hums away in the corner, cooling the air to a springlike chilliness. Lavender and vanilla tickle the inside of my nose. Christ, it even *smells* nice in here.

Wright moves past me and plants himself in the chair behind the desk. He removes his hat, places it on the desktop, then motions to the empty chair facing the desk. "Please, have a seat."

I sit, sinking into the soft leather cushion. Wright stares at me without speaking, a faint smile on his face. He's studying me, the same way a poker player does at a big stakes game. Trying to size me up, trying to read if I have any smarts behind my eyes.

So here we go. Stay cool, Indigo.

"How's trade been for you lately?" Wright asks.

"Can't complain."

"We've had a rainy, muggy spring down in Houston. What about up here?"

"About the same."

He shifts in his chair, looks me over again. Raindrops softly patter against the roof's plastic tarp cover. Wright places his hands on the desktop and slowly runs his fingers over the brim of his hat.

Then he lowers his chin and coolly gazes at me. "I won't waste your time with pleasantries, Trader Cruz. I'm sure you'd like to know why you're here."

I nod, keeping my expression neutral while my stomach jumps around like some kind of small animal's inside of it.

"We're in need of a guide."

Guide. The word gives me pause. It's not the request I'd expected to hear. A brain dump on the goings-on around here, yes. A map for safe passage to Conroe, sure. But not *we're in need of a guide.*

I swallow. "A guide to…?"

He coyly tilts his head. "Not terribly far from here. Wouldn't be more than three or four days' work."

Three or four days? That's too far for Conroe. "Where to?"

"Northwest."

"Waco?"

Wright waves his hand. "Heavens, no."

Thank his god—that's a relief. Waco's a Dallasite stronghold. Gun towers guarding the city, streets crawling with loyalist militia, ever-vigilant drones flying overhead. A squad of Fundies would be shot to pieces before they could get anywhere near Waco.

But then, where? Aside from Waco, there's not much to the immediate northwest of here. No natgas fields, nothing worth fighting for. Just rolling green hill country that's mostly unpopulated except for a few small trader turfs and a scattering of towns and villages.

"Then…?"

Wright purses his lips. "A bit south of there."

I resist the urge to exhale in frustration. "Reverend Wright, if you want me as a guide, at some point I may need to know the destination."

For a moment he says nothing. "Temple," he finally offers.

Temple. I chew on that. What could he possibly want in Temple? There's nothing there. An old abandoned town next to an old abandoned military base. Nothing but empty, crumbling skeletons of concrete, long since looted of anything of value.

None of this makes sense.

Behind me the door flap rustles. A young man brushes past me carrying a large plate of steaming food. He hesitates a moment, motioning with his free hand toward the reverend's hat atop the desk.

"May I?" he asks, his voice nervous and unsure, eyes cast downward.

"Of course," Wright answers, and the kid carefully moves the hat aside and sets down the plate. Roasted pheasant with a side of steamed okra and small loaf of bread. The smell of it hits me, makes my mouth water. Then I recognize the kid's face from our walk over here. He was the one turning the bird on a spit. It was Wright's meal he was cooking, not his own.

The kid steps backward. "Can I bring you anything else, Reverend?"

"I'm fine, Remi," Wright answers, then pats the kid's arm. "Thank you, son."

The kid leaves and Wright nods toward the empty space behind me. "Fine young man, that Remi."

Starving young man, from the looks of him. And he's not the only one. What's the deal around here? I thought Fundies had plenty of money.

The reverend pulls a knife and fork from a drawer. "We have so many fine young men like him who've answered the Lord's call to serve."

Amen. The call to serve *you* food—the true path of the enlightened. Christ, what is it about these people? About him?

Wright carves off a piece of breast meat and chews it slowly. It's an amazing thing to witness, I suddenly realize: this fat-bellied man in fine clothes, enjoying a nice meal in a luxurious tent, surrounded by a starving, ragged mob armed to the teeth. And yet he doesn't seem the least bit anxious, the least bit threatened. Put anyone else in that chair and they'd get gutted on principle. But not the Reverend Zachariah Wright. The comfortable, confident shepherd among his pandering flock. Amazing, the control he wields over these people, the power.

It reminds me exactly where I stand in this little

negotiation that really isn't much of a negotiation. And maybe that's the point of the whole scene. In this place, among these people, Wright holds all the cards. I've got no hand in this game, no cards even. This game is shark versus minnow, not the kind of game I like to play.

"I can draw up a map for you," I suggest, suddenly inspired by my utter helplessness. "Every bit of detail your people will need. Show them the easiest way to get there, show them where the gunbirds out of Dallas are routed right now so they can steer clear of them."

Wright chews his food, looks at me, unimpressed. Dammit.

"I'm friendly with a few traders up that way," I continue. "I could arrange for food and supplies…"

He chews and stares.

"…at trader rates," I add, rather lamely.

The reverend shakes his head. "I'm afraid a map won't do, Trader Cruz. We need you *there*, in person." He swallows another mouthful, points his fork at me and winks. "But don't you worry, you'll be well protected."

"But, Reverend…" I pause as I notice Wright stop chewing, a flash of anger flickering in his eyes. He's been all nice words and manners to this point, but something tells me I've stepped pretty close to the limit of his courtesy. Which may not *necessarily* be a bad thing. Is he desperate? Do I have an angle here? Or is this just the short fuse of a man who never negotiates, who's not accustomed to hearing anything other than *Yes, Reverend?*

Careful, Indigo. Remember, you're the minnow. Too many unknowns here. That ugly bitch named risk is standing right here in the room with you, smiling at the chance to screw you over.

"But what?" he snaps.

I take a breath, try to ignore the churning in my stomach and the image of desiccated heads on spikes. "But I'm not a military guide. I'm no good with guns and weapons. I've never been part of a militia outfit."

He nods in appreciation, or mock appreciation. I can't

tell which. "Not your area of specialty. Is this what you mean to say?"

"Yes, I guess so."

"A lover, not a fighter?"

"Not a fighter, I suppose."

He places his fork and knife down on the desk. "They tell me that bean-eater Guzmán has some witch in his employ out west. They say she can spot a crooked trader just like that." He snaps his fingers to punctuate the sentence. A grin slowly stretches across his face, and it's not the friendly kind he greeted me with earlier. "I wonder what she'd make of you right about now?"

I don't say anything.

Wright stands, puts his hat on. "Come with me."

*   *   *

"Are you a religious woman, Trader Cruz?"

There's no way to answer Wright's question. I'm pretty sure Wright doesn't want to hear my take on the greatest scam ever devised, so I keep my mouth shut.

The sprinkling rain continues as he leads me across the camp. The fallen pine needles, damp and softened, no longer crunch underfoot; now they feel like a spongy carpet covering the forest floor. The same pair of bodyguards trail us, but this time they're joined by the kid who served Wright his meal.

Wright chuckles. "You don't have to answer, of course." He looks me over, as if he's searching for some kind of clue. "Catholic parents, I take it? Dark hair and dark eyes usually means a Catholic heritage."

I don't answer.

"But not you, correct?" he asks. "I've never met a competent trader who had any sense of the divine. And from what I hear, you're a competent trader."

Not much gets past this preacher man.

We walk on, passing by his soldiers, each of whom

stops to bow their head in deference or bid him good day. Men and women, young and old. Every face glows with reverence and awe, with pure adoration.

Zealots, the lot of them. I don't think I've ever used that word before, ever applied it to another human being. But it's the only word that conveys their expressions, the discomforting intensity of their gazes.

I want to ask where we're going, where he's taking me, but my gut tells me to shut up and I'll know soon enough. *You're a fool, Indigo. Why did you think even for a minute this was going to be a straight-up negotiation?*

The tents thin out as we move beyond the camp and deeper into the woods. A sick feeling inside me grows, snaking itself through my insides.

"Ours is a divine endeavor," Wright says. "Sanctified by the Lord. I know that may be hard for you to believe."

We come to a small clearing where two large tents stand side by side.

Wright goes on. "And it's my privilege to serve this sacred covenant between Christ and his people."

As we get closer to the tents, someone from inside yelps in pain. I stop in midstep.

Wright turns to me. "It's a blessing, you understand? Serving my brothers and sisters." Then he furrows his brow in concern. "Trader Cruz, I worry about your soul."

I swallow. Another cry from the tent. This time I recognize the voice. It's Shooter.

The reverend narrows his eyes at me. "All this time and you haven't once asked about your people. Not a single word of concern." He shakes his head woefully. "Shame, Trader Cruz. Shame on you. Even the lowliest of God's creatures looks out for their own kind."

He nods to the guards behind me. One of them nudges me forward. From inside the tent, someone opens the door flap and Wright goes inside. A shotgun pokes my lower back, urging me to follow.

I step inside and there's Shooter, slumped over in a

chair, hands tied behind his back. His left eye is swollen and nearly closed, his lower lip split. A globby mess of blood and spit covers his chin. Two huge men hover over him.

Wright removes his hat. "The trader's life is the road to perdition, Indigo Cruz. Money, money, money. That's all a trader holds dear, isn't it? Closing the deal, making the trade, collecting those pellets."

"Indigo," Shooter mumbles, his voice slow and slurring like a drunk's. He looks up at me, his eyes dull. One of the hulking men punches him and tells him to shut up. I look away. For a moment it's quiet, nothing but the pitter-patter of raindrops against the plastic tarp above our heads.

"But something tells me you're not a completely lost cause," Wright continues. His voice is still cordial and calm, as if we're still chatting over his lunchtime meal, as if we weren't standing three feet away from a scene of cruel violence.

Another man enters the tent, carrying a folding table. He nudges me out of the way, squats down, then unfolds the legs and places the table in front of Shooter. As he's leaving the tent, the man hands something to Wright. The reverend mutters a thank-you, then turns to me. In his hand is an old rusty hammer.

"I believe you still have a heart down there somewhere in that chest of yours, hardened though it may be," Wright says. "I believe you can still be redeemed." Behind him, one of the men grabs Shooter's wrist and forces it onto the tabletop. The other holds the kid from behind in a bear hug. Beaten senseless and barely conscious, Shooter doesn't resist.

Wright raises the hammer, a mad glint in his eyes. "And that's what I'm offering you: redemption. Not a deal, not a trade, but the glory of contributing to the holiest of causes. Trader Indigo Cruz, I'm offering you the redemption of your very soul."

He whirls around and brings the hammer down,

striking Shooter's outstretched hand with a powerful blow. The kid jerks to life, howling and instinctively trying to yank himself away. The two men bear down on him, holding him in place as he struggles, his feet kicking out, boot heels slipping against the ground and finding no traction.

I grind my teeth, try not to react. He wants me to break down, to beg him to stop. He wants me to know this is only a taste of what he'll do to me if I don't play along.

Wright raises the hammer again, strikes Shooter's hand a second time with a sickening thud.

"Stop him, Indigo!" Shooter cries. "Make him stop! Please—"

A third strike, then a fourth. Long wails of torturous pain follow each meaty blow. I want to cover my ears, close my eyes, turn and run out.

The reverend turns to me, breathing heavily, his face splotched red and little beads of sweat spotting his forehead. He looks at me expectantly, waiting for me to plead with him to stop hurting the kid, to say I'll do anything he wants.

That's when something inside me disconnects, goes cold.

Fuck this guy. I fold my arms across my chest, give Wright my emptiest poker stare. He looks at me for a moment, then furrows his brow, confused. I wonder what he's thinking right now. Maybe he's thinking he was wrong about me. Maybe I don't have a heart. Maybe I am beyond redemption. And maybe this poor kid whose hand he's beating into a bloody pulp chose the wrong trader's turf to learn his craft in.

I keep my face an unblinking stone. Once they know they can break you, then that's it. You're their bitch forever.

Behind Wright, Shooter sobs and begs the men to please please let him go. It's a tough break for Shooter. But that's the way of the world, and best he learn that ugliness now. There are torturers and sufferers. Hunters and prey. Winners and losers. If you don't choose which one to be, sure as hell somebody else will choose for you. And if all it takes is a shattered hand to learn that lesson, Shooter can consider himself lucky.

Wright frowns at me, disgusted, then turns back around and raises the hammer again. I hold my breath.

"Reverend Wright!" someone calls out, freezing him in midstrike. I turn and see the shadow of someone outside the door flap.

The reverend lowers the hammer to his side. "What is it, Remi?" he barks.

"He just radioed in, Reverend. He's a few miles out. Be here any minute."

The violence fades from Wright's face. He drops the hammer to the ground, then pulls a handkerchief from his jacket pocket and wipes sweat from his forehead. "Thank you, Remi," he says, his tone shifting instantly back to that of the courteous gentleman. "I'll be along shortly."

He puts on his hat, winks at me. "Please excuse me, Trader Cruz, but there's a matter that requires my attention. We'll continue our conversation shortly."

Wright exits the tent and I finally let out the breath I've been holding. Shooter moans and cries. "My hand, my hand, oh God."

I can't bring myself to look.

*　　*　　*

In the tent next door, I sit on the ground with the same two guards from the ambulance ride watching over me, both brandishing shotguns. Through the thin canvas walls I hear Shooter sobbing convulsively. "It hurts, it hurts." One of his torturers snaps at him, telling him to shut up, and then the cries die down to a whimper.

I try to block out the glimpse I got of his hand as they ushered me out. Blood splattered all over the table, spotting the tent walls, grotesquely twisted fingers attached to a raw, oozing lump of flesh he'll never use again.

Breathe, Indigo. Clear your head. Think your way out.

"Hey," I say to Old Testament.

"Whaddya want?" he answers, narrowing his eyes, tightening his grip on the stock of his shotgun.

"What's going on? Who just radioed in?"

His expression softens. "Prayer Donovan, that's who." He says the name again, reverently, almost a whisper. "Prayer Donovan."

Prayer Donovan?

"I thought he retired?" I say.

He shrugs. "That's what everybody thought."

I lean forward. "So what happened?"

The guard nods enthusiastically. "He come back, that's what."

"Jeremiah," warns Genesis.

But his partner's too excited, too revved up to stop. "He come back for a grand crusade. Them heathens ain't gonna know what him 'em after Prayer's done with 'em."

"Really?" I lift my eyebrows, encouraging him to go on.

"Lord be praised, yes. And you get to lead him into glory, trader. You oughta be honored to be asked such a thing by the reverend."

"Jeremiah!"

Old Testament stops talking, shrugs. "What're you griping at me for? I ain't telling her nothing she don't already know."

"Let the reverend do all the talking," Genesis chides. "It ain't your place."

"Fine," Old Testament grumbles, his enthusiasm smothered.

Prayer Donovan, the infamous heathen-killer, here at this fanatic camp with Reverend goddamned Wright. And me smack in the middle of it all. *Christ, Indigo, what have you gone and gotten yourself mixed up in?*

For some minutes I sit there in silence, no sound

except the rain and Shooter's whimpering. Then the rain lets up and Genesis peeks out the door flap.

"Going to relieve myself," he tells his partner. "Back in a minute. No talkin' with the trader, you hear me?"

Old Testament doesn't answer, still sulking.

When the man leaves, I say, "What's with him?"

The guard looks at me suspiciously for a moment, then shakes his head. "Lord only knows."

"Lord only knows," I repeat softly, nodding.

"You mocking me, trader?"

I give him my sincerest gaze. "You think I want to get in more trouble?"

"You got plenty," he says.

"Got that right." I let my vowels twang in my nose, echoing the West Texas accent I hear in the guard's voice, just enough so he notices.

He tilts his head at me. "Where you from, trader?"

"Odessa, originally."

"No foolin'?"

"God as my witness."

He cracks a smile, points a thumb to his chest. "Midland, born and raised."

"Small world," I say.

"Small world," he agrees.

In my head a clock's ticking, counting down. How many more seconds do I have? If his partner's taking a shit, a nice long shit, I might have enough time.

"Can I ask you something?" I let the question float out of my mouth cautiously, as if I'm scared or embarrassed to voice it.

He hesitates before answering. "Go on."

"Does all this Jesus stuff really work for you?"

There it is, lying out there. It's a clumsy, obvious ploy, but I don't have time for much else. Now it's up to him, and he'll either take the bait or see the hook. What kind of fish are you, Old Testament? The smart kind or the dumb kind?

Long, uneasy moments pass as he stares at me. Then his face slowly changes and he smiles, shaking his head at me as if I'm a poor lost fool. "Why, of course it does."

Good. He's the dumb kind.

I scoot a bit closer to him. "But how can you be so sure?"

He squats down, looks me squarely in the eyes, taps his chest. "You let Christ into your heart and you can feel it, deep down."

"Really?" I scoot closer.

"Really." His eyes sparkle with pious joy. "When I accepted Jesus as my Lord and Savior, he came into—"

I lunge forward, striking his crotch with my boot heel as hard as I can. He makes a muffled grunting sound, drops the shotgun, then falls to his side, both hands cupped over his balls. I scramble over him and put him in a choke hold from behind, pressing my forearm into his throat, wrapping my legs around him so he can't wriggle free.

He struggles, tries to break my grip. Old Testament's strong, hard to hold. He manages to free one leg, but I quickly trap it again. I press my arm further into his neck so he can't get any air, can't call out for help. He grabs my arm, scratches at it, trying to free himself, but I'm locked in deep.

Finally his grip weakens and then his body goes limp. I keep the choke in place for a few more seconds to make sure he's out, then I let go.

I grab the shotgun and peek out the door flap. No sign of his partner yet.

I step out of the tent slowly, scanning the camp in the near distance. A few people milling about, but they're too far away to notice me. I hope.

My footsteps make no sound thanks to the rain-moistened ground. I step around the tent lightly, scanning the grass and dirt until I see the telltale imprints on the forest floor. The barest traces of the other guard's tracks.

The trail leads into a thicket some fifty feet away.

Shooter sobs from inside the other tent. I pause, grit my teeth.

Get yourself out of here, Indigo.

I crouch down and follow the tracks into the thicket. For once today, luck favors me as I reach the dense clump of trees and bushes. The guard's busy trying to squeeze out a shit, squatting with his pants down, facing away from me. I creep up behind him, letting my boots fall silently on the ground.

I'm nearly on top of him now. I reverse the shotgun in my grip, holding it by the barrel. The metal is cold and slick in my hands. I have to hang on tight.

"Psst," I whisper, and the man whirls around awkwardly, nearly toppling over. I swing as hard as I can, cracking him across the jaw with the stock. The shotgun slips from my hands on the follow-through, flying through the air and disappearing into the undergrowth. I spin off balance and fall backwards, my back hitting the ground.

I scramble up to my feet. The guard lies still on the ground, his pants down around his ankles. Out cold.

I quickly go through his pockets, find a pair of keys. My truck's keys. Another lucky break.

All right, Indigo. Go find your ride.

CHAPTER 3

The last direction I want to go is back toward camp, but that's exactly where I'm heading. Every animal instinct in my body cries out for me to run as fast as I can into the woods, to put as much distance as possible—as quickly as possible—between me and these lunatics.

But on foot they'd catch me inside of ten minutes. You've got to find your truck, woman.

I circle around the edge of the camp, ducking and crouching behind shrubs and thickets, keeping out of sight. I've got a minute, two at the most before one of my guards recovers enough to call for help.

Tents and campfires and Fundies with guns: that's all I see as I skirt the camp's perimeter. With each passing moment, the voice telling me to make a run for it grows louder, more insistent.

About thirty yards ahead of me, a motorboy sits on his bike, its engine idling as he chats with a woman with long braids and a two revolvers in hip holsters.

There's a shout from somewhere in the distance, and they whip their heads around toward the sound. A man's voice.

"She's gone!" the voice cries out. "The trader's gone!"

Crap.

I bolt from the thicket toward the motorboy and the woman. They're still looking the other way when I reach them, and I bury my shoulder in the woman's gut at full speed, knocking her backwards.

"What the—?" is all the motorboy gets out before I'm on top of him. He's young and slight of frame and caught off guard. I yank him off easily and send him sprawling across the ground.

I hop on the bike, gun the engine, and pop the clutch, leaning forward as the bike lurches into gear. I speed away from camp, the engine screaming through the gears in rapid succession, reaching fourth before I hear gunshots behind me. One hits a tree on my left and wood splinters fly into my face. I crouch low over the handlebars, trying to make myself a smaller target.

I steer the bike side to side between the trees, which gets trickier as the forest becomes more dense. Weeds and undergrowth slap violently against my shoes and pant legs. A blur of greens and grays and browns whizzes past my head. The bike's an old Kawasaki 150, its size and weight similar to the Honda I had as a kid. I haven't been on a bike in years, but handling the machine comes back quickly. I shift my body back and forth, counterbalancing the bike's weight. Movements I suddenly remember as if I'd never forgotten them.

I look over my shoulder, don't see anyone following yet. I turn the bike sharply, changing direction. The little engine roars, stinging my ears with its high-pitched squeal.

Think, Indigo, think.

Then there's a *POP-POP-POP* from behind me. I look back. A pack of motorboys, too many to count at a glance, have appeared from nowhere. I whip back around, catching the bright burst of muzzle flashes at the edge of my vision. The air's suddenly filled with howl of engines winding up and down and the crackle of gunfire.

The ground's slick from the rain. I push the bike as fast

as I can, feeling the tires lose traction in a wet patch—a stomach-dropping here-we-go sensation that lasts half a second—then catch again on drier ground. I try to keep my head down, leaning so far forward the handlebars pound against my chest like someone's punching me.

Think.

POP-POP-POP.

I come up out of a ditch, landing in a large puddle and nearly upending the bike, when I notice something to my right. The broken remains of I-45 about a hundred yards away, twisting and turning northward in a familiar pattern. Suddenly I'm oriented. I know where I am.

I gun the engine, heading straight for the highway. The forest thins then disappears altogether as I approach the old interstate. I'm out in the open, an easier target now. But if I make it to the other side of 45, I'll find Jones Creek, swollen and swift-running from the recent rains. And along the creek there's a maze of trails and hiding places I know like the back of my hand. I can lose them there.

As I speed toward the ex-highway, I steal a backward glance, see the first of the motorboys coming out of the forest. I turn back to the bouldered concrete and rusted rebar coming into focus. A sickening realization hits me. I have to slow down to get through this mess.

The bike's gearbox screams its complaints as I downshift quickly and decelerate, scanning for a path across the snarl of rubble, much of it hidden beneath a thick blanket of switchgrass. As I slow down, the roar of the engines behind me grows louder with each second. I stand on the foot pegs and stretch out my neck, squinting, looking for a clean way through. *POP-POP-POP-POP.* The shots hit a slab of concrete next to me, sending a spray of dust plumes high into the air.

No time, Indigo.

I point the bike between two fractured pieces of road and grit my teeth, zooming across the interstate, expecting at any moment to snag a tire on rebar or upend the bike on a hidden piece of road. Halfway through, the handlebars suddenly jerk up and back as I hit something hard, bottoming out the front shock, sending vibrations and a sharp pain through my wrists and arms. It's a struggle to keep my grip, but I manage to keep the bike upright and moving. More gunshots crackle behind me.

A moment later and I'm through, barreling down the embankment for the cover of the forest. I reach the trees and take a quick look back. The first ones coming across hit something hidden in the underbrush and wipe out, causing a chain reaction behind them. Bikes flip riderless into the air, others collide into a chaos of bodies and machines.

I slow to a stop behind some trees and watch, shielding my body behind a large oak, taking a moment to gather my wits and orient myself. Back at the highway a pair of riders slowly pick their way around the mess, straddling their machines awkwardly as they step their bikes through.

I put the bike into gear and turn toward Jones Creek. As I come around a thick wall of pines, something huge and white juts out in front of me, and the bike slams into it hard. I fly forward, my legs hitting the handlebars, flipping me through the air.

Ground, trees, sky. Ground, trees, sky.

I slam into the ground and tumble forward, my arms and legs flopping around like a rag doll's. Then the world around me settles and I'm lying in damp grass. The trees in front of my face seem to be growing sideways. For a second there's no sound and no movement, then I gasp as if I've been holding my breath underwater for a long time. I'm aware of pain in my legs—my thighs feel like two large, pulsating bruises—and a dull, throbbing ache in my neck.

Twenty feet away there's a white truck. The bike I stole lies in a mess beside it, smoke wafting up from the engine, front wheel folded in half from the impact.

A pair of boots step in front of my vision, inches from my head. Soldier's boots. I crane my neck and look up. At first there's two of him, then my eyes regain focus and I see a man leaning over me, hands on strong thighs. He's thick-limbed and muscular, and even through my woozy haze I can feel a raw physical power emanating from him, like a bull bred for fighting.

"You're not going die on me, are you?" he asks in a gravelly voice.

He wraps a huge hand around my upper arm and gently lifts me into a sitting position. "Take a minute. Catch your breath."

My entire body hurts. I shake my head, try to clear the cobwebs. In the distance I hear the whine of motorbike engines. Panic surges.

"I've got to get out of here," I mumble, my speech slurring like a beat-up fighter. I try to get up, but the man's heavy hand on my shoulder keeps me in place.

"You stay right there," he says.

A pair of motorboys approach, stopping abruptly at the truck. Their engines idle as they stare at us, strange looks on their faces, as if they suddenly don't know what to do.

The man straightens up and turns to face them. "I've got her. Go on back to camp."

They stare at us, mouths hanging open. My head clears a bit more and I realize they aren't staring at *us*. They're staring at *him*.

"Go on, now," he says, his voice rising a notch. "I've got her."

The motorboys look at each other, then put their bikes in gear. "Yes, sir," one of them defers. "Thank you, sir," the other one adds.

The man turns back to me and I get a clear look at his face, at the large letters branded into his forehead. They read JESUS SAVES.

*   *   *

The truck rocks back and forth over uneven, rain-softened ground. Shocks squeak, ancient sheet metal rattles. I sit in the passenger seat, my body sore and head throbbing, but otherwise unhurt. The driver next to me doesn't speak. I steal glances at him, this legend of the Fundie cause. His bulky frame barely fits into the driver's space. A thick shock of cropped black hair sits atop his head, flecked with gray around the temples. Only his face gives away his age, a looseness around the jowls under a salt-and-pepper beard, wrinkles spreading out from the eyes. Early to midforties, I guess, roughly the same age as me. His arms and shoulders, oddly, aren't a patchwork of tattoos like the others back at camp. Aside from the branded letters running across his forehead, his massive body is unmarked.

"So you're Prayer Donovan?" I ask, finally breaking the silence.

He takes his time answering. "Mm-hmm."

"Heard you retired," I say. The rumor on the trade channels was he'd gone hermit, packed it up and moved east to the Big Thicket. No one really knew why, though.

Another long silence. "Who says I didn't?"

We roll along at an even, unhurried pace. My window's down, door's unlocked, and there's no one around, but Donovan doesn't look the least bit concerned I'll escape. He didn't even bother to bind my hands. If he were anyone else I'd say it was a stupid oversight, but Prayer Donovan isn't anyone else. He knows that trying to run from him would be pointless, that his reputation is more than enough to keep me in place. He knows I'll stay put. We both know it.

He turns the truck up the embankment toward I-45. Out my window I see the deep dent in the front quarter panel where I crashed into the truck. The ground levels out as we reach the top of the slope, then Donovan maneuvers the truck carefully through the gauntlet of concrete debris and twisted steel. My head throbs.

We get through to the other side and roll down the embankment, then he points the truck south, keeping us parallel with the highway. I rub my temples, trying to block out images of Shooter's mess of a hand, dreading a worse punishment when we get back to camp.

"This mission to Temple," I say, trying to take my mind off what awaits me, "that's why you're here?"

For a brief moment, I see a flicker of surprise on his face, but it's gone quickly. "Who told you that?"

"Wright did. He wants me to be your guide."

Donovan doesn't say anything.

"So what's in Temple?" I ask. What's so important that they had to call the great Prayer Donovan out of retirement?

He grunts, and his stony expression doesn't change. "You tell me, trader. Seems like you know more than I do."

"We didn't quite get to the details," I say, swallowing as I see a scattering of tents through the trees. Camp.

"Before you ran out, you mean?" Donovan adds, turning the truck toward camp.

A crowd quickly forms around us. Dozens of men and women gawk at Donovan as he slowly moves the vehicle through a throng of slack-jawed admirers.

He brings the truck to a stop next to a large tent. "Didn't give them kids you left behind a second thought, did you?"

I don't say anything, wondering how he knows about the greenies. They must have radioed him about us.

"Shameful," he says, shaking his head, "running out on them like that. They didn't deserve that."

"I watched your reverend hammer one of their hands to a pulp," I blurt out. "I guess that's what they deserve, is it?"

Donovan snorts. "Reverend's got his reasons."

Go fuck yourself, Fundie.

He exits the truck and disappears inside the tent. Two men appear outside my door, scowling. "Get out, trader."

I step out and they grab me, clamping my upper arms in viselike grips. They jostle me around the truck and shove me through the tent's door flap.

I stumble inside to find Reverend Wright embracing Donovan.

"So *good* to see you, son," Wright beams. "Lord above, what a joy it is to lay my eyes on you, my boy." The reverend backs up a step, holds Donovan by the shoulders. "As God is my witness, I thought I might leave this earth without seeing my blessed Prayer Donovan again." He wipes a tear from his cheek.

It's a world-class performance. The fat preacher would have made one hell of a trader.

Behind them stands a tall, thick-boned woman with long braids that reach her waist. She watches the exchange between the reverend and Donovan, a sour expression on her face. Her eyes are small and dark. Her shiny black hair is streaked with gray. She looks over at me and scowls. Affixed to the canvas wall behind her is a large map of the Republic.

"Good to see you too, Reverend," Donovan says, his tone polite and restrained, a counterpoint to the preacher's frothy enthusiasm. Then he nods at the woman. "Sister Zara," he says flatly.

"Thank you so much for coming, son," Wright gushes. "Please, sit down."

Wright settles in a folding chair, one of four arranged in a circle. Donovan and the woman follow suit. Wright looks at me coldly. "Welcome back, trader." He motions to the last empty chair. "So happy to see you've joined us again."

CHAPTER 4

Donovan and the reverend spend the next few minutes exchanging pleasantries and catching up. The reverend asks him about the hunting in the Big Thicket. Donovan, clearly not the talkative type, answers in short, clipped sentence. Not bad. Can't complain. I reckon so. I sit and listen, keenly aware of my hands and fingers, recalling the sounds of a hammer striking flesh and bone. My thoughts drift to the greenies. I wonder if they'll all end up like Shooter, tortured and maimed.

Wright leans forward, placing his hands on his wide thighs, his expression earnest. "Prayer, the Lord has delivered an opportunity we cannot fail to act on. And we must seize this opportunity swiftly." He tilts his head toward me. "This trader, Indigo Cruz, will serve as your guide to Temple and back."

Donovan looks at me, shakes his head. "Infidel guide, Reverend? Ain't there some other way?"

"If we had any other path, Prayer," Wright continues, "believe me, I'd take it, but hers is the biggest trader turf in the area. She knows these parts backward and forwards. She'll be able to get you there quick, and she'll keep you clear of those flying guns out of Dallas."

"She can't draw up a map?" Donovan asks.

Now you're talking, Brother Prayer.

Wright purses his lips, shakes his head. "That was my first thought as well. But this mission's too important to place our faith in a mere scrap of paper. If she travels with you, she'll keep you out of harm's way, seeing as that's the only way she'll keep *herself* out of harm's way." He gives me a knowing look, lifts an eyebrow. "Trader Indigo Cruz has a keen sense of self-preservation, as we've all just witnessed."

Donovan exhales audibly. "I don't like it."

"It don't matter if you like it or not, soldier," the woman, Zara, snaps. "The reverend's word is consecrated. Ain't your place to question."

Donovan meets her gaze, giving her the same condescending look I give a greenie when they say something stupid. The look only infuriates her more.

"Ain't your place to question," she repeats, sneering, her torso rigid and angled forward as if she might burst out of the chair at any moment and pounce on him. Neither of them blinks or speaks as the tense moment stretches, then the reverend raises a conciliatory hand, a father settling a fight between bickering children. "It's all right, Sister Zara. We're all here doing the Lord's work, are we not?"

After a moment, Zara leans back into the chair, chastened and fuming. "Yes, Reverend," she grunts.

The reverend glances at me. "Well, perhaps not *all* of us," he says, and a sliver of a wry smile bends one corner of his mouth.

"All right, then," the reverend continues, slapping his palms against his thighs, "let me get right to it." He stands and moves his overfed bulk to the map on the wall.

"Reverend," Zara says, lifting her chin at me. "The trader don't need to know the particulars."

"You're right," the reverend agrees, then motions to the door flap. "Trader, if you would excuse—"

"The more I know now," I cut in, "the more I can

help." It's a bit of a gamble, speaking out of turn, but I want to know what the game is, what I'm about to get thrown into.

The reverend looks annoyed at the interruption, but then he purses his lips and considers what I've said. He lift his eyebrows at Donovan. "Prayer?" The branded one scowls at me.

"Maybe there's something I know," I suggest before Donovan can say no, "something it's better to know now than when we're on the road." I have no idea what that something might be, of course, and I only half-expect them to buy it. I haven't exactly proved myself to be the most reliable partner so far.

"She's an infidel," Zara seethes, "with a forked tongue." *Right on both counts, lady.*

Wright ignores Zara's comment. "Prayer?" he repeats.

Donovan eyes me for several moments. Finally he shrugs. "She's gonna find out soon enough. The more we know now, the better."

"What if she runs again?" Zara growls. "She'll just go and tell—"

"I trust you'll keep a close watch on her so that doesn't happen, Sister Zara," the reverend interrupts, with a finality that says the question's been settled. I can stay and listen.

Wright turns back to the map, then with his finger makes a large circle around southeast Texas. "This is our sphere of influence, as I'm sure you're all aware. The seed of our faith has taken root, grown, and flourished, thanks be to God."

Sphere of influence. It occurs to me this is the perfect phrase to describe the area he's indicating. That's because it's not Fundie *turf*, not technically. Every major city in the area—Houston, Galveston, Beaumont—and a large swath of the Gulf Coast, from the Louisiana border stretching west to Port Lavaca—is controlled out of Dallas. But that's just in name only. Everyone knows the show is really run by the Fundies and for the Fundies. Wright has his faithful installed in every police force and governing body in the southeast; his fat fingers pull on countless strings of countless puppets. And in the few places where he doesn't have a reliable go-to, he exerts his will with bribes and violence like some old-style mafia boss. In just two decades, Wright's influence has expanded steadily and relentlessly, an aggressive cancer invading organ after organ. Town by town, city by city, port by port, the reverend's managed to gain control of the greater part of the Gulf Coast.

Opinions vary as to why Dallas has let the reverend's power grow unchecked. On the trader channels some say the Dallasites have grown too weak and lazy. Others claim there's a secret alliance between the capital and the reverend. Then there are those who insist the Dallasites are only waiting for the perfect moment to take Wright out. Until this morning I never gave the matter much thought. The politics of the faraway never helped nor hurt my trade out in the wastelands.

Wright motions toward the left side of the map. "In the west, that godless desert snake has driven countless souls from their homes, forcing them to flee east."

That's a new one. I've heard of Ernesto "El Flaco" Guzmán called many names, none of them complimentary, but this is the first *godless desert snake*.

"And they've settled here," Wright continues, tapping a blue spot, "at Lake Conroe, where they've found refuge and safety in numbers. As many as ten thousand from what we understand."

Ten thousand? There's been talk of "thousands" on the trade channels, but I'd figured two thousand, tops. But *ten thousand*. Even if it's only half that, it's as much as a medium-sized city.

"You can imagine the conditions of the camp there," Wright says, "the suffering, the hunger, the deprivation." He shakes his head, his expression one of practiced, expert mournfulness.

"Trader," he says to me, "you've heard about the relief mission, I assume, on your shortwave channels?"

Donovan and Zara turn their eyes to me, expectation on their faces. I clear my throat. "Nothing specific. Rumor is a UN convoy will be heading down soon."

"You know when?" Wright prods.

I shake my head. "Nobody knows. All they're saying is soon."

"So no one's seen anything yet?" he asks. "None of your trader friends have spotted a convoy coming over the border?"

"No," I answer truthfully. A relief mission for ten thousand would be huge. Dozens of trucks. Not the kind of thing that would be missed.

Wright nods. "Good. So there's still time."

Time for what? Where is he going with this? Earlier he mentioned Temple. I don't see how Temple fits into what's going on in Conroe.

Wright goes on, speaking to Donovan now. "A week ago, Sister Zara took a scouting party northwest of here. They spotted a large congregation of vehicles at the old army base near Temple."

Okay, now we're getting somewhere.

"How many?" Donovan asks.

"We counted seven hundred fifty," Zara answers. "Trucks, cars, motorbikes, all war-outfitted and ready to go. And more was coming in every hour."

No one speaks for a long moment. It's a large number of machines to be gathered together, unusually large. A rolling army of steel and guns.

"Guzmán," I mutter, the thought dropping from my brain to my mouth. "He's going to raid the UN convoy." A relief mission of that size would carry a wealth of supplies, fuel, and food. A tempting target for anyone with enough manpower and firepower to take it.

Wright wags a finger at me. "That was *exactly* what I

thought, trader. But that's not the case. It's a raid on that convoy, sure enough, but the desert snake isn't the one behind it."

Confusion. If not Guzmán, who else could it be? Aside from Guzmán or Wright, I can't think of anyone who could manage to amass so many vehicles for a convoy raid.

"Who, then?" Donovan asks.

"The Unaffils," Zara answers.

The *Unaffils*? That's a hard one to swallow. For the better part of twenty years, I've traveled and traded throughout the unaffiliated territory, that huge swath of land in Central Texas that neither Dallas nor Guzmán nor the Fundies control. It's a place with little in the way of natgas basins, so it's been left alone for as long as I can remember, probably since before Secession. Those who don't live there call it the Big Empty, a sparsely populated, worthless hinterland of small towns, isolated hermits, and little else. The Big Empty is the last place you'd expect *any* kind of cooperative undertaking to happen, much less a large-scale raid on what's likely to be a heavily armed, well-armored convoy out of the States.

"I don't see it," Donovan snorts, crossing his arms. "The Big Empty's just a whole lot of nothin'."

Exactly.

"The intel's solid," Zara counters.

Donovan grunts. "So you say."

"The intel's solid, Prayer," Wright insists, before Zara can argue back. He moves over to the braided woman, places his hand on her shoulder. "Zara's party...*questioned* a couple locals who were on hand, keeping watch over the fleet. She asked them all about it, and we're reasonably sure they answered her truthfully."

I can imagine. Questions asked with fists, hammers, and machetes. Answers mumbled through blood and broken teeth.

Wright goes on to explain the rest of the intel Zara came back with: how the Unaffils got wind of the UN mission to Conroe (apparently the worst secret in the Republic) and decided to band together for a one-time raid on the mother of all relief missions. For weeks they've been quietly, patiently assembling a war party that probably numbers a thousand vehicles by now. It takes me some time to wrap my mind around it, but the more I chew on it, the more it makes sense. Unaffils are isolationists by nature, but they're also opportunists. Anyone who's traded there could tell you that. So it doesn't take a big stretch of imagination to see them pooling their resources for a once-in-a-lifetime payoff.

"Trader," Wright says, "you hear anything about this on your shortwave?"

I shake my head.

Wright stares at the map, gravely nodding his head. Then he turns to Donovan. "Brother Prayer, we can't stand by and do nothing. We can't let them deprive all those starving families from much-needed relief." There's an urgent quality in his voice, an insistence that's just short of pleading. It's like he's *selling* the idea to Donovan, trying to convince his soldier the mission is worth coming out of retirement for, worth risking his life over. If I weren't seeing it with my own eyes, I never would have believed that Prayer Donovan—the tip of Wright's spear for decades—needed anything more than a word from his master's voice to take on a mission.

But Wright's mission of mercy is anything but that, of course. His plea to Donovan is an obvious sham. Obvious to this heathen, at least, as I study the map on the wall. He couldn't give a damn about those families and what they're going through. He's a power-mad expansionist, no different than his brown-skinned rival out west, and the refugee camp at Conroe is an easy grab that pushes his "sphere of influence" outward. A ten-thousand-person buffer on your northern border isn't a bad thing to have, not to mention the influx of wealth from the UN convoy that's on the way. A land grab with fringe benefits.

Then again, maybe he only wants the relief mission goodies for himself and screw the refugees. Maybe he'll wait for the UN convoy to leave, then take the booty at the point of a gun and head back to Houston. That's the racket border bandits work up north, when smaller convoys drop off aid at the smaller refugee camps along the Oklahoma border. When the UN trucks head back to the States, the minute they're out of sight the bandidos come out of hiding and plunder the camp, leaving the poor starving bastards worse off than they were before.

But this is *Reverend Zachariah Wright*, I remind myself. It's hard to see him taking the money and running, not when there's ten thousand fresh souls he can convert. And after all the hell those refugees have doubtless been through, odds are they'd welcome him and the safety of his protection with open arms.

Whatever his motives may be, the Unaffils and the fleet they've put together are Wright's big complication, the wild card he has to remove from the game. That's why Prayer's here, why he's been called out of retirement, though it looks like he needs some convincing to carry the Fundie flag again. His devotion to his preacher isn't nearly as zealous as the folklore would have you believe. Not anymore, at least.

"Scores of children, driven from their homes with nothing but the clothes on their backs," Wright says, then pauses dramatically, tightening his lips into a sad grimace and shaking his head. "The horrors they've seen in their long journey across the wastelands, I shudder to imagine."

He lays it on thick, setting the whole thing up as a sacred crusade, a call from God. "Even the most sinful among us," he preaches, motioning to me, "have been called to serve on this holiest of endeavors."

You silver-tongued devil. It's a dig so clever, it almost makes me like the old crook.

"So how long will it take us to get there?" Donovan asks, eyeing the map.

At this implied acceptance, the reverend's posture relaxes and relief washes over his face. It's the look of a man who's just received the good news he'd been hoping for, but the arrival of which was never a certainty. Wright wasn't sure Donovan would help, it seems clear, until this very moment.

The preacher approaches Donovan, places his hand atop his shoulder, smiles down at him. "Thank you, son."

Donovan replies with a single downward motion of his chin. The bow of a loyal soldier.

*   *   *

They feed me some kind of bird meat stew, a tiny portion that does little more than tease my hunger. I eat it greedily in a tent, sitting on an old cot with a moth-eaten wool blanket bunched up beside me. My humble accommodations are surrounded by half a dozen guards who look like they'd love nothing more than to see me make a run for it so they can take me down like a quail flushed out of the bushes.

We leave for Temple in the morning.

I try to sleep, but my restless, uneasy mind doesn't let me. I think back to the last time I found myself among Fundies, a few years ago. It was a trade run down to Houston. I hadn't been there in a long while, since before Wright had taken full control of the city. I'd heard all the talk about the fanatics' tight grip over the city, about the wariness of outsiders, but I'd also heard that Fundies dealt square, and when it came to business they traded fair. Shotgun McQuinn told me over the shortwave that he'd safely traded with the Fundies plenty of times, and that more often than not he'd turned a decent profit. Not my kind of crowd, Shotgun had told me, but they were all business. After listening to McQuinn, I guess curiosity— and more than a little bit of good old-fashioned trader greed—got the better of me, so I went down there to check things out.

When I arrived, I couldn't believe how things had changed. Under the Dallasites, H-town had been like any other large city: a sprawl of decomposing buildings and houses; a local machine of Dallas loyalists running a corrupt city government and an even more corrupt police force. The barest appearance of civil order was maintained while Dallasite engineers sucked wealth out the ground in nearby natural gas fields and the local cops shook down residents for protection money. Like Austin, Waco, San Antonio, and every other major town in this failed state once known as the Republic of Texas, Houston's sole reason to exist was to enrich the shining, modern capital in Dallas. It was a system that had been in place since long before I was born, and locals in Houston (and everywhere else) had little choice but to live under Dallas protection. The unpoliced wastelands between the cities, those vast expanses of territory that not even Dallas had the resources to control, were untamed, unpredictable, and dangerous. No place to live if you wanted to live long. Of course, there were trade turfs like mine scattered here and there and a few local militias protecting smaller towns and outposts, but these were the exceptions to the rule, the one-percenters who lived outside the fold. Most Texans, for generations, had lived in the cities, poor and hungry and ill-treated but surviving, under the indifferent gaze of their Dallasite overlords.

But as I rolled into Houston, that seemingly unbreakable model had been entirely displaced. Reverend Wright, as the trader gossip went, had doggedly inserted himself into Houston's political and security apparatus, eventually bending the city to his will after years of scheming and bribing and building up a massive following of true believers. There had been no massive uprising, no "revolution day" that marked his overthrow of the city; instead it had been a slow, savvy power grab by small, almost unnoticeable increments. The steady, tenacious growth of a vine that one day finally chokes its host. By the time I returned to Houston on that trade run, it might as well have been a different city in a different country, so total was its transformation. The lack of security that plagued all cities, for example, had been all but eliminated. Houston was, as I came to see with my own eyes, a safe city.

A bit *too* safe for my liking, as it turned out. Where the Dallasites had turned a blind eye to pretty much all criminality that didn't interfere with their graft, the Fundies weren't exactly the look-the-other-way type. They took law and order seriously, and to a deadly extreme. Public executions had become commonplace. During my visit, I saw no less than a dozen hangings each day. Murders, rapists, and thieves dangling from gallows all over town.

And just as numerous were the neck swingers who'd committed "religious crimes." If you blasphemed, they strung you up. If you openly practiced any creed other than the Fundie faith, they strung you up. Out after curfew? Caught drinking alcohol? Take the Lord's name in vain? They had a rope with your infidel name on it. And the rifle-toting, tatted-up religious police were everywhere, on every street corner, watching everyone, zealous in their strict enforcement of Fundie orthodoxy. Servants of the Path, they were called. And as if their suspicious glares and high-caliber weapons weren't enough to keep you in line, huge murals of Reverend Wright—his wide, compassionate, and thoroughly creepy smile beaming down on you—were everywhere, lest you forget who was in charge.

And the rallies! Christ, I'd nearly forgotten about those. Twice daily, at sunup and sundown, thousands would assemble in and around Fundie churches for worship rallies. Preachers with bullhorns, amplified voices shouting fire and brimstone, crowds roaring and cheering. *Death to the infidels! Death to Dallas!* Every last resident seemed to come out, leaving all the buildings, homes, and shops empty. If there was any dissension in Houston, if there were any nonbelievers, I never saw them. The whole city, it seemed, had jumped enthusiastically onto the Fundie bandwagon. The chatter on the trade channels had said as much, of course. When Shotgun McQuinn found out I was heading down there, he'd warned me. *It's a no-nonsense, Fundie town, Indigo, top to bottom and inside out.*

Three days were about all I could take before I had to get out. Too much looking over my shoulder. Too many goddamns and fucking hells I had to swallow down when I spoke with vendors. That kind of thing wears on you, makes you paranoid and twitchy: the awareness that the slightest slip-up will land your neck in a noose. And not a drop of tequila to be found anywhere in that whole city, which is no small thing, either. I headed back to my turf without making a single trade, vowing never to return.

CHAPTER 5

I pass the night sleeping in fitful spurts, which is more tiring than if I'd spent the whole night awake. The rusty cot springs grind and squeak as time passes like a slow-dripping faucet. Finally a purplish haze appears outside and it's morning.

One of the guards enters the tent. "Rise and shine, trader." He makes a follow-me motion with his shotgun.

Outside, my crew's nowhere to be seen; Wright's soldiers have them holed up somewhere, hidden away. Last night before we parted ways, the reverend assured me—smiling in a way that seemed as much a threat as a promise—that when we returned from Temple I'd find them well-fed and (except for one mangled hand) unharmed. He didn't say what would happen if I didn't return or if I failed as a guide. He didn't have to.

It's a chilly morning. I keep the wool blanket wrapped around my shoulders. Wisps of fog creep between tree trunks like some kind of enormous, smoky spiderweb. I'm prodded to move forward by a poke of steel at my lower back. I've got five tattooed babysitters this morning: two in front, three behind me.

All around camp, small groups of Fundies clasp hands

in prayer circles. I catch words and phrases as I pass by.

"This is the day that the Lord hath made," murmurs a young woman with close-cropped hair and rags for clothes, her eyes closed tight.

"Let us be glad and rejoice in it," says a filthy, barefoot boy next to her.

"Let us hear not the pleas for mercy from Thine enemies, O Lord."

"May we tear the heathens asunder as You have commanded, O Lord, cleansing the earth in anticipation of Your return."

"For Thine is the kingdom, and the power and the glory…"

"…forever and ever."

It's a lot to take without coffee.

My minders sit me down next to a campfire, where an old man tends to a large cast-iron pot of the same whatever-bird stew they gave me last night. His brownish overalls might have been blue fifty years ago. Surprisingly, he smiles kindly at me as his veiny, shaking hands pass me a bowl of stew and a tin mug of coffee. Ravenous, I wolf down the food, hardly pausing to breathe. When I finish, the old man dips his ladle into the pot and serves me another bowlful. I eat more slowly this time, feeling the gnawing hunger in my belly start to fade.

When I finish the second bowl, one of the guards says, "Let's go, trader."

I stand, holding the mug with both hands, its heat seeping into my chilled fingers. Warmer now, I shrug off the blanket, letting it fall to the ground.

The soldier in front of me motions ahead. "This way."

As I follow, the old man in the overalls looks up and says, "Have a blessed day, ma'am," smiling a toothless, contented grin.

They bring me to the edge of camp, where there's a line of five vehicles. Three beat-up Humvees and a rusted-out Jeep, each with a .50-cal machine gun turret on top. All of them have the same green-and-brown camo paint job, and behind them sits my old Ford pickup, looking painfully unmilitary. The boy Remi scurries between a supply tent and the vehicles, helping soldiers load food, jugs of water, bags of natgas pellets, and boxes of ammunition. Zara supervises, scowling over every item, snapping orders, telling the loaders where to put what. Next to her stands a girl, maybe a couple years older than Remi, early teens, who could be Zara's twin. Same braids, same scowl, same folded arms.

"Where's the rest of them?" I ask the guard next to me, a woman with shaved eyebrows and a large cross tattoo on the side of her head.

The woman spits on the ground. "The rest of what, trader?"

"The rest of the convoy."

She nods toward the five vehicles. "That's the convoy right there. Ain't no rest of it."

That can't be right. "Wait a second," I blurt, "you're saying *this is it?*"

"That's it," says a deep, familiar voice behind me. I turn and see Prayer Donovan approaching. An M4 carbine is strapped to one of his shoulders, and over the other he's carrying a well-used suit of body armor. A soldier gearing up for a mission.

"Look, I'm no soldier, but isn't that a bit…*light* for a combat operation?"

"Not if you're hauling that," he answers, pointing at two men carrying a large wooden crate between them. "Easy, boys," he calls out to them.

"We got it, Brother Prayer," one of them grunts, grimacing with the weight of the load. They walk slowly, carefully.

I almost ask Donovan what's in the box, but then I don't bother. Its contents are obvious: explosives, and quite a large load of them from the looks of it. More boxes appear, carried and loaded with delicate care into the trucks.

"TNT, ammo nitrate, C-4," Donovan says.

"Enough to blow up a fleet," I murmur, watching them load the trucks. The convoy will be a rolling powder keg. Wonderful.

"The trader catches on fast," he replies. Donovan then nods at the woman with the cross tattoo. "I've got her from here, sister."

"Yes, Brother Prayer." The woman's voice flutters with nervous excitement. She orders the guards watching over me to fall out, and they all leave us to go help load the vehicles.

"Come on," Donovan tells me, tilting his head for me to follow.

We head over to the lead Humvee, where we find the boy Remi at the rear of the vehicle, stacking boxes of ammunition. His face lights up when he sees Donovan. "Morning, Brother Prayer." He wipes sweat from his forehead.

"Good morning," Donovan greets him. "You're Remi, is that right?"

"Yes, sir." The boy beams up at Donovan.

"You making sure that load's balanced, Remi?"

"Yes, sir, Brother Prayer," Remi assures him. He gestures excitedly to the load. "You can check it. I got it spread out all nice and even. Go ahead and take a look."

"I'm sure it's fine, son." Prayer pats the boy on his shoulder. "Looks like a fine job to me."

"These trucks ain't gonna load themselves," Zara shouts. She's standing near the middle of the convoy, hands on her hips. "Get over here and help, boy!"

The boy flinches, peers over at Zara, then back up at Donovan. "She ain't in charge, is she?" he asks, low enough so the woman can't overhear.

Donovan winks at the boy. "Think I woulda come along if she was?"

Remi smiles, nods knowingly.

"Get over here right now," Zara barks, stomping her foot.

The boy shrugs. "Guess I got work to do."

Donovan nods. "Better get on it, then."

"Yes, sir," the boy replies, throwing back his bony shoulders and sticking out his chest in what he must imagine is a soldierly way. Then he returns at a run to the procession of loaders.

After he passes by her, Zara approaches us, followed by her little twin. Frowning, she looks down at my hands. "Why ain't the trader bound?"

"She ain't going nowhere," Donovan replies.

"She can't be trusted, Prayer." Just Prayer, she calls him. Not *Brother Prayer*.

He swings the truck door open. "Didn't say I trusted her." He throws his gear onto the front seat.

"She oughta be tied up," Zara's sidekick sneers.

Zara whirls around and slaps the girl hard on the jaw, sending her sprawling to the ground. She glowers down at her. "What have I told you about speaking out of turn?"

The girl stands up slowly, a clump of grass in her hair, head down and eyes lowered. "Forgive me, sister," she mutters. There's no crying, no trembling, just a dull-eyed downward stare. The kind of grim acceptance you see in a dog that's come to accept a regular beating as its lot in life.

I glance over at Donovan. He's glaring at Zara, his lips drawn in a straight line, jaw clenched tight.

The branded one points a finger at her. "Don't touch that child again."

Their eyes lock and she doesn't flinch. There's not a flicker of fear in her expression. I take a step backward.

"My ward, my responsibility," she hisses.

"And this is my war party," he says, pulling rank. "And you'll do what I say."

She doesn't have a quick answer for that one, but she doesn't back down, either. The activity around us has come to a stop. Soldiers frozen in place watch the standoff with anxious expressions, supply bundles in their arms. I take another step back.

Neither of them blinks or moves.

After a long, tense moment, Zara finally collects herself and inhales deeply through her nose. She nods slowly. "As you say, brother." Her words are obedient, her tone and expression anything but.

She turns stiffly and makes her way down the line of vehicles, the punished girl following in her wake. The soldiers go back to the business of loading supplies.

I exhale and unconsciously bring my hand to my chest, disappointed as I realize I don't have my flask of tequila. Donovan kneels down to sort through a box of ammunition, and I move around to the back of the truck, where Remi's bringing up water jugs.

The boy shakes his head, makes a quiet whistling sound. "That was a close one."

"The girl," I say, "is that her daughter?"

"Miriam? Nah, she's an orphan like me. Zara takes care of her."

That's one way of putting it. "So, Prayer and Zara. They have some kind of bad blood?"

The kid leans over the tailgate, but can't push the jugs far enough in. "Here," I say, "I got it." I hop up into the rear of the truck and slide the jugs snugly against the rest of the load.

"Thanks," Remi says. He takes a sneaky look behind us, then turns to me, keeping his voice low. "Zara and Prayer are brother and sister in Christ. There ain't no doubting that."

I sit down on the tailgate, nodding. "Of course."

"But they don't see eye to eye on much," he continues. "Zara didn't want the reverend to call on Prayer. Says he don't have the righteous fire in his eyes no more. Says he's gone soft."

"Doesn't look too soft to me," I say, truthfully.

"Me, neither," the boy agrees, his expression

brightening. "We're blessed he come back. Truly blessed, trader. Them infidels ain't gonna know what him 'em."

I lean in a bit. "Say, Remi, did you pack my radio yet?" I ask the question as casually as I might ask about the weather.

His smile fades. "Radio?"

"Yes."

"Brother Prayer or Sister Zara didn't tell me to bring no rad—"

"Lord, Remi," I laugh, "what good is a trader without a radio?"

Doubt clouds his face. I haven't been around the boy enough to know how gullible or how stupid he is. I'll find out in the next few seconds.

I tilt my head at him, a teacher addressing a dimwitted student. "How are we going to know if they changed the drone routes if I'm not checking the trade chatter?"

Behind us, Donovan's inspecting the turret atop the second Humvee. He's paying no attention to our conversation, his full concentration focused on the task at hand.

I shrug. "Go ahead and ask Brother Prayer if you want."

I leave the suggestion hanging in the air, letting him think about it. He looks over at Prayer, then back to me.

"I think it's over yonder," he finally says. He leaves and disappears into a tent near the end of the convoy. When he emerges moments later, he's carrying a burlap bag over his shoulder.

The boy approaches and swings the bag from his shoulder, then holds it out for me.

I stare at it for a moment, wondering where I can hide for a few moments to sneak a call back to my turf and let them know what's happened.

"Thanks, Remi," I say, reaching for the bag. Before I can grab it, a hand seizes my wrist.

"What do you think you're doing, trader?" Prayer

growls.

I grit my teeth, don't answer. My arm feels like it's in a vise. He squeezes harder, then twists my arm in a way it doesn't appreciate.

"Just wanted to check the battery," I gasp.

Donovan glares at the boy, who's still holding out the bag at arm's length.

"She said she needed it to…" His face drops in shame before he finishes the sentence, realizing how ridiculous it must sound. He lowers the bag and looks to the ground. "I'm sorry, Brother Prayer."

Donovan torques my arm further. I groan as pain shoots up to my shoulder.

"This one's got the devil's tongue," Prayer scolds. "You don't lift a finger for her unless I say, you understand?"

I can't see the boy's reaction. I'm doubled over awkwardly, my cheek pressed against the rough steel of the truck bed.

"Yes, sir," I hear him answer.

Donovan wrenches my arm upward and backward and now there's nothing but pain and the sickening sensation of my elbow and shoulder joints forced beyond their limits, ready to snap at any moment.

"Good morning, all," a third voice says. The pressure on my arm lessens a bit.

I twist my neck around and see Wright smiling down at me. "Making friends this morning, are we, Trader Cruz?"

"She was trying to get hold of a radio," Donovan accuses.

"Well, let's give it to her, then," Wright declares. "Prayer, let her go."

Donovan releases me and my arm drops, thudding against the truck bed. My shoulder throbs and my arm feels like a wet noodle.

Wright nods to Remi. "Hand her the radio if you will, my boy."

The kid takes a nervous glance at Prayer, who looks as

confused at Wright's comment as I do.

The reverend smiles, seems unconcerned. "Go on," he urges gently.

Remi squats down and pulls the shortwave out of the bag. He stands and presents it to me.

"Ah, just one little thing," Wright adds, then he tugs on the microphone cable, disconnecting it from the transceiver. "There we are." He tosses it to the ground, then winks at me. "You can listen to the chatter all you want, but we can't have you talking to your friends in that trader tongue no one can make heads or tails of, can we now?"

I guess not. "Put it on the front seat," I tell Remi. The boy carries the transceiver to the front of the truck.

Wright moves down the line of trucks, all smiles and jokes and two-fisted handshakes. King Zachariah inspiring his troops.

They finish loading the vehicles over the next half hour. Zara oversees everything, barking orders and double-checking supplies. The girl Miriam follows her like a shadow. The hangdog expression from her beatdown is gone as she mimics Zara's scowl and echoes each order.

When the loading is completed, Wright lines up the soldiers shoulder to shoulder. By rank, it seems, with Donovan at one end and Zara next to him, then about a dozen more of the tattooed faithful, ending with Remi at the far end. I count fifteen men and women, fifteen pairs of sharp, determined eyes. None of them—aside from Donovan and Zara—strike me as older than thirty. Again I chew over the small team Wright's assembled, over the odds of our success. One in ten? One in a hundred?

Just get them there and back, Indigo.

I watch as the lined-up soldiers kneel down and bow their heads. Wright takes his hat off, gives it to one of his bodyguards, and approaches Donovan. He bends down, taking Donovan's head in his hands, and presses his forehead to Donovan's. Wright squeezes his eyes shut and speaks in low, soothing tones. It's a prayer, a soldier's blessing, or some such nonsense.

When he finishes, Donovan stands, his eyes glistening, the stone face cracking with fissures of emotion.

Wright then moves to Zara and performs the same ritual. She's instantly overcome with emotion, bawling and clutching onto the reverend's forearms. He finishes with her and she stands, her face red and blotchy, tears streaming down her cheeks.

One by one Wright moves down the line, reducing each of the soldiers into a sobbing mess as easily as someone else might flip a light switch.

Last he reaches Remi, who's visibly shaken even before Wright finishes with next-to-last Miriam. With Remi, Wright does more than bend down, he actually kneels, lowering his bulk down onto two knees as he grasps the boy behind the neck and presses their foreheads together. He stays with the boy longer than he did with the others— maybe twice as long—and prays with more fervor, more intensity. The others stand in line, heads bowed and eyes closed.

Finally it ends, and Remi stands up with puffy eyes and snot dripping from his nose that he wipes with his sleeve. Bodyguards help the reverend to his feet, and one of them brushes grass and dirt from the reverend's pant knees. Wright dons his hat and spreads his arms out wide. "I wish you all Godspeed, brothers and sisters. May the Lord watch over your journey."

An ancient Humvee with darkened windows rolls up, as if on cue. A bodyguard opens the mud-spattered door and Wright climbs into the backseat. The truck rolls away and disappears into the forest.

"Load 'em up," Donovan tells Zara, and she repeats the words to the squad, amplifying the order into a screeching shout. The soldiers scramble into action, whooping and hollering in a sudden burst of eagerness. Inside my chest, my heart thuds with dread. *Here we go.*

Donovan motions for me to come. "Move it, trader," he cries impatiently.

"Ain't no standing around, heathen," a woman yells as she hops into the driver's seat of a Humvee.

"Yeah, this ain't no market haggle in Nacogdoches," a shirtless man covered in tattoos calls out, closing the door after the woman and climbing onto the running board. A pair of barbed wire crosses hang from nipple rings, jiggling back and forth as he shouts, "This here's real work. THE LORD'S WORK!"

"AMEN!" someone up front cries, followed by a gunshot. A chorus of amens answers, as does a volley of shots fired into the air. Wild hoots and the crackle of automatic gunfire fill the forest.

Just get them to Temple and back.

I make my way around to the passenger side of my truck and get in. Donovan sits behind the wheel; the shortwave radio is on the seat between us. As the deafening chaos of bloodthirsty shouting and guns discharging explodes all around us, he nods at me, his sidearm still holstered, his expression cool. The calm center of the Fundie storm.

Donovan keys the ignition and the engine rumbles to life. Then he slides open the window behind the seat. "You ready back there?"

Remi stands in the bed, wearing a crisscross of ammo belts that hang loose over his bony chest. "As God as my witness, Prayer Donovan, I surely am!" He bangs his fist on the roof and howls.

Prayer smiles at this, but only for a moment. He bows his head, closes his eyes, mumbles something. Then he opens his eyes again and waves his left arm out the window. In the front Humvee, Miriam sits in the turret. She sees Donovan's signal, returns it, then slaps the roof of the truck. The lead Humvee rolls forward and one by one the convoy vehicles follow.

The war cries and gunfire die down as we move

through the pine forest, our pace quick and steady. There's a large spiderweb crack in the passenger side-view mirror, and in it there's a kaleidoscope picture of rows of tents and a group of onlookers waving goodbye.

I watch as the broken image of the camp grows smaller, then disappears.

CHAPTER 6

The racket a shortwave radio makes can be downright annoying if you're not used to it. And from the look on Prayer Donovan's face, he's not used to it.

I turn the knob slowly, searching through the frequencies, listening for keywords. It's slow going. I hear nothing but squeaks and squawks, pops and static, with the occasional gurgle of Spanish or English, none of it traderspeak.

We've been driving for maybe an hour. The truck rocks back and forth over uneven, grassy and sometimes muddy plains. It's green all around, the kind of vibrant green you see only after a thunderstorm when the sun is bright and the sky is cloudless but the terrain is still soaked. We work our way around enormous copses towering pines, thick with impassable, head-high undergrowth. Between these dense forests lie huge expanses of switchgrass fields, populated by sparse scatterings of oaks, their wide canopies standing lonely and separated from their neighbors by hundreds of yards. It's one of those *in-between* terrains, where the vegetation can't seem to decide whether it wants to arrange itself as Central Texas plains or South Texas thickets.

The convoy weaves its way through the landscape like some giant segmented insect, its Humvee head a half mile in front of us. I turn the radio knob and listen. Squeaks and squawks, pops and static.

"Does it have to be that loud?" Donovan asks.

"Yes." I turn up the volume a bit, even though I don't need to.

He grunts his displeasure. "You been listening for twenty minutes. You ain't heard nothing?"

"Sometimes it takes a while."

I've forgotten how radio noise can drill a hole in your ear. I don't really hear it anymore, haven't for a long time. After a few years your mind starts to sort through the unimportant sounds like you might scan through an old book, thumbing through the pages and ignoring the blur of words until you arrive at the chapter number you're looking for. And so far I'm not finding anything. The radio chatter is silent. To my ears, anyway.

Donovan sighs. "How long's a while?"

"Maybe an hour." And sometimes longer. Trader communications have been a hide-and-seek game with the Dallasites since before I can remember. We settle on a frequency, then they find it and jam it up, so we move to another. Round and round it goes like a dog chasing its tail.

Traderspeak is under constant change as well, with new code words and phrases replacing old ones all the time, continuously evolving to keep the Dallasites in the dark. There's no pattern to any of it, which is why the Dallasites—despite all their money and tech—are always two steps behind.

I keep listening. Squeaks and squawks, pops and static.

An hour later, I'm about to give up when I finally hear something. Chatter so faint, so hidden by static that I nearly passed it by.

I lower my head, turn my ear to the speaker.

Donovan notices. "You getting someth—"

I hush him with a forefinger to my lips. I close my eyes and concentrate, blocking out the rumble of the motor, the squeak of the shocks, sending it all to the back of my mind, focusing on the almost inaudible chatter of traders coming from the speaker.

Code words and key phrases begin to come through, forming the complex lattice of traderspeak, as different from normal language as a web is from a single strand of spider's silk. Using ten words where one will do, talking around things, implying the subject, never directly mentioning it.

I squeeze my eyes tight and listen, trying to recognize the voices. It sounds like Sanchez from the panhandle and Shotgun McQuinn. Sanchez carries most of the conversation, as usual. He's always been a chatty one. Eventually the dialogue starts to take shape, and a subject emerges from the babbling chaos.

Conroe. They're talking about the refugee camp at Lake Conroe. And the supplies that will soon be on the way. The mother of all relief missions. A fleet of UN trucks carrying supplies. A gold mine on wheels.

And then suddenly they stop, and the speaker emits nothing but static. I sigh and straighten back up in the seat.

"What was it?" Donovan asks.

"Not much. The tail end of a conversation."

The heat of the morning sun grows warmer through the windshield. The truck moves over a flat field, and for a few minutes the constant jarring is replaced by a smooth glide. This is what it must have felt like when they had real roads and highways stretching straight and unbroken to the horizon in every direction, back before they cracked and came apart and all but disappeared in the overgrowth. Houston to Temple in a matter of hours, pedal to the floor, instead of a day-and-a-half trudge in low gear across the open wastelands. Better days.

I go back to working the knob, scanning the airwaves. "So why the kids?" I ask.

"What?"

"The kids." I point my thumb over my shoulder toward Remi. "I got greenies in my turf, but I don't ever bring them along on anything important."

He snorts. "I was younger than any of them when I started crusadin'."

"But you're Prayer Donovan, they're not."

"They got talents, otherwise they wouldn't've been picked."

"Talents for what?" I turn the knob. Squeaks and squawks, pops and static.

"Recon mostly. Them young'uns can climb a tree quicker than a squirrel. Up in the high branches, they can see for miles around."

He speaks earnestly—or is it defensively?—almost as if he's trying to convince me that children crusaders aren't anything unusual. Then it occurs to me that maybe it's not me he's trying to convince.

I motion again toward Remi, standing in the truck bed behind us. "And what's his special talent? Let me guess. Code breaking? Military strategy?"

Donovan seems to suppress a laugh.

"Really, why'd you pick him to come?" I press.

His expression darkens. "Didn't say I picked him." He says it more to himself than to me.

"Who did?"

"The reverend, Sister Zara."

If it were up to me I wouldn't have brought the kids. He doesn't say it, but that's what I hear.

We drive on and hours pass. The ground's dried out now and the sun blazes, searing and relentless. The sky is brilliant and blue and empty except for a few wisps of clouds, survivors that managed to somehow avoid boiling away in the oven heat of late afternoon. My forearms are damp with perspirationand sweat runs down my neck and chest. We trudge along at twenty-five miles an hour, too slow to generate a cool breeze, only a warm push of air against my face like hot breath.

I check the radio every quarter hour, but don't pick up any more chatter. I try not to think about the greenies, try to stay focused on the job, reminding myself it's an easy gig, all things considered. Between Huntsville and Temple, there's nothing but trees and plains. Not a single major city or established turf in our path, so we don't have to worry about getting shot at for trespassing or about paying off townies or turf bosses to pass through their territory. And drones coming out of Dallas aren't anything to sweat over, either. It's been months since any gunbird paths have veered south of Waco, a fact the Fundies are obviously unaware of, otherwise they wouldn't have been so desperate for a guide. All the drones coming out of Dallas these days head due west, attacking or spying on Flaco Guzmán, whose land grab out in the desert has the Dallasites worried. Trade chatter says the crafty warlord's been shooting gunbirds out of the sky as fast as they can send them out. God bless that old crook for giving me one less thing to worry about.

Of course, if this were any other kind of convoy, we'd have to worry about the everyday hazards of the open wastelands: road bandits, highway gangs, and your usual bands of roving crazies. But this is a *Fundie* convoy, and everybody knows Fundies fight to the death with smiles on their faces, and they won't think twice about blowing themselves up before they let a heathen get the better of them. Any would-be hijacker with half a brain would steer clear of our little train as soon as they got a good look at those tattooed bodies manning the gun turrets.

So things could be worse, I suppose. We're even making good time. Temple by nightfall is looking more likely by the minute.

But even as I tell myself these things, when the convoy comes to a dead stop, it feels inevitable.

*   *   *

"It's the axle," says the woman with the cross tattoo on her scalp, kicking the dead Humvee's tire. "Busted clean through."

Zara stands next to her, hands on hips, staring at the broken front end of the Humvee. Steam escapes from the sides of the hood, and water streams onto the grass from the bottom of the cracked grille.

Donovan lies belly-down on the ground, inspecting the damage. Then he stands up, shakes his head grimly at Zara.

Cross Tattoo stares at the ground. "I'm sorry, Brother Prayer, Sister Zara," she mutters, then bites her bottom lip. "This is Satan's work. He's up to his old tricks again, trying to keep the faithful from their duty."

"Satan wasn't driving," Zara sneers, "was he?"

The woman doesn't raise her eyes from the ground. "No, sister."

Donovan motions toward the second damaged Humvee, some fifty yards back. "What about the other one?"

The girl Miriam runs up. "U-joint," she pants. "It's gotta be replaced."

The boy Remi arrives at a jog a few seconds later.

"What was it?" Donovan asks him.

"Old building foundation," he answers. "Big chunks of concrete, sharp rebar all over the place."

The Humvee on point had rolled right over it, the unseen hazard covered by a thick carpet of grass, and destroyed its axle. The driver of the second Humvee, keeping what should have been a safe distance, hit the brakes too late.

Donovan's mouth forms a tight line. "Take all the supplies and gear out of this one," he tells Remi, pointing to the broken Humvee, "and divvy it up 'tween the others."

He places his hand on Cross Tattoo's slumped shoulder. She raises a heavy head to look up at him, her eyes full of shame and tears.

"Weren't no avoiding that, sister," he says. "Ain't no use worrying about what's done."

She nods. "Yes, brother." Her voice cracks.

"Get that U-joint off your truck and put it on that other one," he orders. "Go on, now."

"Yes, brother."

The squad springs into action like a disturbed ant mound, redistributing the lead Humvee's load and positioning jacks with long handles under the carriages of both vehicles to begin repairs.

The three working Humvees and my truck are positioned around us, forming a square. Pairs of soldiers stand in each of the turrets, scanning the flat landscape with binoculars.

I approach Donovan. "How long?"

He checks the sun's position, squints. "We're gonna have to camp here tonight."

It's not the answer I was hoping for.

*   *   *

While the idea of spending the night in the unprotected wastelands doesn't go down well, I can't deny it's a far better option than traveling after sunset.

Night travelers are easy pickings. All you need is a good ambush spot, night vision gear, and a murderous disposition.

There are those who attempt a night run, of course. The stupid or the desperate, usually. And nine times out of ten they don't live long enough to see the sun come up.

Donovan might have decided to risk it. The convoy's got a lot of firepower and our night vision gear's decent enough. But something tells me the loss of one Humvee was enough bad news for him for one day. And traveling at night—even slow and careful and heavily armed—is a dicey matter at best. The odds favor hunkering down and waiting for dawn.

While one team works the vehicle repairs, another sets up a secure perimeter. I watch as they unload the gear. Motion sensors, night vision goggles, portable microphones with parabolic dishes. All the equipment's beat up and dented and well used. Obsolete, decades-old throwaway tech smuggled in from the States.

The teams work quickly, efficiently, and in silence. Zara frowns over every detail of the Humvee repair, while Donovan walks the perimeter. I lean over the front of my truck, where I have an old map with frayed edges spread out on the hood. I study the contour lines, crunch distance and speed numbers in my head. After a while I start to lose the map's details in the falling light. I look up and see the sun dropping low on the horizon, a swollen, bloody orange.

A couple hours later, the Humvee's U-joint is finally replaced. Its donor vehicle with the broken axle sits some distance away, lying in the tall grass like the skeleton of some huge fallen animal, its meat and skin picked clean by scavengers.

Dinner is cornbread, bean stew, and dried meat, though what kind of meat is hard to say. Coyote or feral hound, maybe. Two large iron pots hang over a fire and the sweet smell of mesquite smoke fills the night air that's finally, mercifully gone from warm to cool. After a prayer from Zara that gives thanks to everyone but me and Satan and lasts the better part of a century, the food's doled out into metal bowls and passed around. About a dozen Fundies sit on the grass around the fire eating; the rest patrol the surrounding darkness or stand sentry in the turrets.

They make small talk, campfire talk, chatting about how dry the weather is this far north and what the hunting prospects might be.

I'm excluded from the conversation, which suits me

fine, until Remi asks, "So where're your people from, trader?" He wipes stew from his chin.

Zara shoots him a foul look. "Don't matter where she's from, does it?" she snaps.

The girl Miriam sits next to her, her scowl a perfect copy of Zara's. "Don't matter one bit," the girl echoes.

Zara slaps the girl hard on the back of her head. "Eat your dinner," she scolds.

"The trader's from Philistia," the man with nipple rings grunts. The Bible humor goes over my heathen head, but it draws snickers from the others.

"McKinney," I answer.

"McKinney?" Nipple Rings exclaims. "Why, you're almost a Dallasite, then."

I shrug.

He eyes me sideways. "You got any kin in Dallas?"

I shake my head as I gnaw a tough piece of meat. No kin in Dallas. No kin anywhere.

"Lord almighty," the woman next to him says, "of course she don't got kin in Dallas, you fool. You think she'd be a trader out here in the wild if she had rich kin in Dallas? She'd be up there countin' her money, drinking fancy wine, waited on hand and foot by robot slaves." The woman makes a mocking face and sips from an imaginary glass, her pinky finger raised high.

Chuckles from around the fire.

Nipple Rings waves a hand dismissively. "Traders love money as much as Dallasites. Probably more." He nods at me, grins knowingly. "Ain't that right?"

I don't say anything.

His smile fades. "Ain't that right, trader?" he insists.

Conversation stops and everyone looks at me, waiting for an answer. In an instant the air's become heavy and tense. I glance over at Zara. She's grinning at me, delighting in my discomfort.

Nipple Rings glares at me, leans forward. "'Fess up, now. You'd swap your own kin for a bag of pellets, wouldn't ya?" The little crosses dangle from his chest, shining in the firelight.

Your own kin for a bag of pellets. I wince inside, stabbed in an old wound I'd almost forgotten about. A sudden anger wells up, overcomes me.

I grit my teeth, stare back at him. "I'd trade you for half a bag."

His mouth drops open.

"But nobody would be fool enough to pay that much for a stinkin' Fundie," I add.

The soldiers gasp in unison.

Zara springs to her feet, her plate toppling to the ground. Her eyes are wild, crazed. She balls up her hands into fists, trembling with rage. An insult from a heathen is more than she can bear.

She takes a step toward me, then freezes, her gaze shifting to something behind me.

"Showing off that trader's charm over dinner?" I turn and look up. Prayer Donovan stares down at me, shaking his head. "Leave you alone for ten minutes and you already got 'em at your throat."

Zara wavers for a moment, then snorts and sits back down. "Good-for-nothin' infidel," she grumbles.

Donovan sits, and Remi appears at his side with a steaming bowl of stew, topped with two large pieces of cornbread. The branded one takes the bowl, thanks the boy. The air around the campfire settles into something less charged, overcome by Donovan's cool, collected presence.

"Now what could you have said to set Sister Zara off like that?" Donovan asks.

"Just about anything," I answer, glaring over at her. *Fuck her, fuck Nipple Rings, fuck all these brainwashed fools.*

I breathe deeply, dropping my eyes to the ground in front of me, trying to calm myself. *Work the job, Indigo. Don't they hate you enough already? There's no point in making things worse for yourself.*

Donovan takes a bite of cornbread. Remi sits next to him, watching him with intense admiration, a dog waiting for the slightest attention from its owner. The kid's awestruck.

The conversation slowly revives as the meal continues. Low murmurs, nodding heads, the occasional chuckle.

"Don't make it harder on yourself," Donovan warns me, his voice low so only I can hear. He keeps his eyes fixed on his bowl, raises a spoonful of beans to his mouth. "Most of my brethren would kill you soon as look at you."

I let a long breath slide out between my teeth. "You think you can actually pull this whole thing off? Because I don't see it."

He looks at me, firelight flickering over his face, over the burn scars in his forehead. "Ain't nothing for you to worry about, trader."

"Meaning I should shut up, or meaning it's not a high-risk mission?"

"The shut up part." Donovan takes a long drink, then wipes his mouth with his sleeve. He hands the cup to Remi. "Would you mind getting me another, son?"

Remi pops to his feet, takes the cup. "Yes, sir." He scrambles away.

Donovan stands and unhooks a hand radio from his belt. He fiddles with the knobs for a moment, static popping and hissing, then brings the radio close to his mouth.

"Post one check in, over," he says, then waits for a response.

Moments pass. "Post one check in, over," he repeats, a bit louder. He waits, but there's nothing but static.

He lowers the radio, squints out into the darkness, searching. Then he reaches out a hand behind him. "Specs," he barks, and a moment later a ponytailed soldier rushes over to him with a pair of night vision goggles.

The soldier starts to hand them to Donovan, but suddenly drops them to the ground. Then the soldier doubles over, clutching his hand to his stomach. He looks up at Donovan with a strange, confused look on his face. In the next moment the back of the soldier's head explodes and his body falls limply to the ground.

"SNIPER!" someone shouts, and everyone drops down, bellies flat against the grass. For a moment I stare dumbly at the dead soldier, his blood and brains oozing across the dirt.

"Get your heathen head down!" someone shouts, and I dive to the ground. There's a loud hiss as someone douses the campfire with water, and then it's completely dark.

"I'm hit," someone cries out.

Suddenly the air crackles with automatic gunfire, and far out into the night I see muzzle flashes flare and disappear like fireflies.

It's an ambush.

"Where are they?" someone shouts. I think it's Zara, but all the sounds are distorted by the blood pounding in my ears. I press my body against the grass. Green tracers light up the night, passing inches over my head.

A chaos of yelling and returning fire erupts.

I look over at Donovan. He's hollering at me, pointing behind me. Time slows and reality bends and stretches. It takes a moment for me to understand what he's saying.

"Behind the truck!" he's shouting. "Get behind the truck and stay down."

I keep my stomach flat against the ground and wriggle across the grass to the Humvee. Bullets ping and thud against the vehicle's body. I crawl past a tire as it's hit. A whistle-hiss of escaping air blows the smell of warm rubber on my face. The vehicle lurches and then settles, leaning at an angle atop the flattened tire. I move around to the back of the truck, gunfire ringing in my ears.

Between bursts of shots, there's frenzied screaming and cries for help from the wounded. I peek around the side of the truck, try to see what's happening. In the flash illumination of muzzle fire, I see bodies all around. Dead

Fundie soldiers scattered across the ground.

My mind whirls and I fight to control the panic surging through my body. I squeeze my eyes shut and press my head against the ground. Bullets penetrate the Humvee's chassis with pounding thuds.

Think, Indigo!

Get up and run, you're probably dead. Stay put, you're also probably dead. These are not good options.

I reach up and crack open the Humvee's door. I move my hand around the floorboard, the seat, searching for anything that might help: body armor, a weapon, a radio. Then my hand runs across the barrel of a pistol. I grab it and pull it down to the ground. In the darkness I can't see it, but it feels like a 9mm.

Better than nothing.

I look behind me, opposite of the ambush. Tracers zoom and disappear into the black of night. The gunfire grows louder, more intense.

When in doubt, run like hell. I flick off the gun's safety and take a couple deep breaths, rising up and readying myself to run as fast and as low as I can for as long as I can.

A flash of white light, brilliant and blinding, swallows everything around me, and a tremendous thud hits my head like a sledgehammer.

Then, just as quickly as it appeared, the light winks out and the world goes black and quiet.

CHAPTER 7

Warm metal against my cheek.

It's the first sensation I'm aware of when I start to come around. My vision blurs and drool leaks from the side of my mouth.

I take a few deep breaths to try and clear my head. It doesn't help much. My mind is a fog, my head throbs painfully.

At some point I realize I'm lying on my stomach. I move one arm, the other, then both legs. I carefully wiggle my torso, lift my neck. Nothing seems broken, but everything's sore.

As I lift myself up, my surroundings lurch and spin sickeningly. My eyeballs feel loose and heavy in their sockets and only partially under my control. *Deep breaths, Indigo. Take it slow.*

I manage to rise up into a sitting position, my body complaining with every movement, then I look around. I'm in a cramped, enclosed space with corroded metal walls and a low ceiling. All around me lie Fundie soldiers in various stages of consciousness: the kids Miriam and Remi, both still out cold, their arms and legs splayed out like discarded dolls; Nipple Rings and a pair of Fundie soldiers coming around, blinking and flailing their arms in slow motion, like boxers who've just been knocked out; Zara on her hands and knees dry-heaving, her unraveled braids hanging like frayed curtains alongside her cheeks. It's dark, the only illumination coming from a small battery-powered light hooked high up on the wall.

"It was a nighty-night," a voice behind me says. I turn—slowly so my heavy eyeballs don't lag behind—and see Donovan sitting with his back to the wall. His arms are folded across his chest; he looks as if he's been waiting for some time for the rest of us to wake up.

I nod, wiping the spit off my chin. Nighty-nights are stun grenades, the heavy-duty kind that pack a monster punch. I once saw a trader knock out forty head of cattle just to show a buyer how effective they were. They're very good trade, those little flash bombs, fetching a high price for anyone foolhardy enough to smuggle them in from the States. Pain shoots through my head.

"Who?" I ask, closing my eyes and rubbing my temples.

"Don't know," he answers.

"Where are we?"

"Semitrailer." He motions toward the doors. "Locked in."

The air stifles inside the large metal box. It's so warm it must be well into the morning already. I wonder how long I've been out.

Zara leans against the wall, her forehead shiny with sweat. "This is her treachery," she croaks, pointing at me. "Trader whore double-crossed us."

Sure. I planned the ambush. It was an especially genius maneuver, especially the part where I had them nearly kill me.

"You're a damned fool," I snarl.

Donovan shakes his head at Zara. "It was an ambush, plain and simple. Weren't her doing."

The kids stir and groan, then slowly wake up. Remi sits up and pulls his knees to his chest. He blinks slowly, a line of drool suspended from his chin. Miriam crawls over to Zara, who grabs the girl under the arms like a baby and props her up against the wall. The girl rests her head on Zara's shoulder and quietly sobs. Zara pulls the girl close, strokes her hair and wipes tears from her cheeks. "It's all right," she coos. "I'm here, sweetie. I'm here."

Outside, a man shouts. I can't make out the words, but the tone has the air of authority. Someone giving orders. Next there's a clanking noise against the trailer, then the door swings open and sunlight pours into the space, blinding me.

"Out," a shadow standing in the doorway barks. I place my hand to my forehead to cut the glare, and my eyes adjust enough to see the large-caliber rifle in the man's hands. He swings it at us, gesturing impatiently. "I said get out!"

My legs wobble as I stand and gingerly step forward, pressing my hand against the wall to steady myself. Someone helps me down out of the trailer, and I'm blinded a second time by a brilliant midday sun. The someone then pulls me by my upper arm and hustles me away from the trailer. I squint, my eyes tearing with the sudden brightness. "Stay there," a woman's voice grunts as she lets go of my arm.

Moments later my vision settles into focus, and the first thing I see is the last of the Fundie soldiers climbing down out of the trailer. Our captors line us up shoulder to shoulder. Donovan stands between me and Zara. Beyond the trailer I see the remains of our camp, where three burned, blackened Humvees sit still smoldering, and among them most of the Fundie squad lies dead. In the near distance I count four more trailers like the one we just exited, and beyond them there's a chain-link fence topped with razor wire, encircling a small collection of trucks, Jeeps, and four-wheelers. To our right, a dozen old mattresses are strewn about the ground. On top of them, people are fucking, their dirty bodies grinding into each other. Others mill about in the spaces between the mattresses, browsing like shoppers in a market, pausing when they see something that interests them, then stripping out of their soiled fatigues and joining in. They seem to be oblivious to us and the smoldering carnage nearby. The little talk I hear sounds closer to animal noises than human speech. Grunts and cries and slurring laughter. Drugged out of their minds, all of them.

With a shudder of dread, I realize who's caught us.

The man who let us out of the trailer approaches, holding an M6 carbine at the ready. He's covered head to toe with dirt and grime, so much it's impossible to see what his skin color is. His long hair is a matted mess of reddish orange. He's wearing a hunter's vest packed with ammo and tattered fatigues. Around his neck runs a thick cord of rope, hanging almost to his belly, heavy with a collection of human ears. Most of the trophies on his necklace are dark and shiny and hardened, hardly recognizable. Others, the freshly gathered ones, still have a pinkish color and a hardened crust of dark, dried blood along the severed edge. Behind the ear necklace man, and equally filthy, stand two men and two women also brandishing semiauto rifles.

"On your knees," Ear Necklace orders.

No one moves.

I glance over at Donovan, notice others doing the same, waiting to follow his lead. His hard eyes stare through Ear Necklace as if he's looking at some point fifty miles beyond.

"Down," the man says, lifting the rifle and moving his finger inside the trigger guard.

Donovan lowers himself to his knees. The rest follow, except the girl Miriam. She remains standing, jutting her chin out in a burst of defiance.

"The righteous don't kneel for no heathens," she challenges.

She barely gets the last word out before she's shot

below the knee. Her lower leg snaps grotesquely and she collapses to the ground, howling and writhing in agony.

Zara makes a move toward the girl, but Donovan wraps his arms tightly around the woman's shoulders, keeping her in place. Zara struggles to break his grip, but he's too strong. "My girl," she cries. "My girl."

"Fresh mouth," Ear Necklace growls, smiling. "Hope the rest of her is just as fresh." He nods to one of the men, who then comes over and picks Miriam up, throwing her over his shoulder like a sack of rice. The girl passes out and her body goes limp, a sticky rivulet of blood leaking from her leg to the ground. The man carries her like a prize deer, trudging toward one of the trailers.

"Where you taking her?" Zara shouts. Then she turns to Donovan, pleads with him. "You can let them take her. You know what they'll do to her."

They'll do what men always do, I think grimly. Reveal themselves as the monsters they really are.

I watch the man stomp up the trailer ramp with the girl bobbing listlessly over his shoulder. With his free hand the man opens the door and they disappear inside.

*   *   *

They sit us down on the grass in front of the semitrailer where they took Miriam. I notice a smokestack poking up from the roof, the kind you see on a barbecue, and from it a plume of gray smoke wafts steadily upward. The familiar aroma of burning mesquite fills my nose. The sun blazes down bright and brutal, frying the exposed skin on my arms, face, and neck. The scattering of mattresses is behind us, unseen but heard, the grunting and groaning only yards away.

"Send that one over to the mattresses," someone behind me cries, their voice garbled and sloppy like a drunk's. "The one with the nice ass."

"No, not her," a woman argues. "Send the big boy. I

wanna see what he's packing."

Two men approach, carrying a large wooden table, which they place between us and the trailer. Another brings a wide bench and sets it down. The three take great care in the arrangement, making several adjustments before wordlessly agreeing on the correct distance between bench and table. One of them produces a frayed, stained tablecloth and gently lays it over the tabletop, then ceremoniously smooths out the wrinkles. Another takes out cutlery and plates, placing them down carefully.

The trailer doors open outward with a screeching creak. A dark cloud of smoke pours from the opening, and a large man emerges out of it. A demon released from the gates of hell, who goes by the name Dealer Valdeez.

Valdeez stomps down the trailer ramp, his colossal bulk making metallic stamping noises with each step. He's larger than I remember, which I wouldn't have thought possible, and he's completely hairless, with dark red paint covering his head and face. His brows, ears, and cheeks sport dozens of silver and gold ring and stud piercings. Covering the top half of his torso, which mostly consists of a pair of enormous fat man's tits, is a rusting mesh of chain mail. The wide girth of his belly spurts down and out from the bottom of it, and aside from the chain mail and his body jewelry, he wears nothing else, not even shoes. At the outer edge of his cave-like navel, there's a tarnished silver ring piercing the size of a dog collar. A length of chain hangs down from the ring, then loops upward again, presumably connected to some part of his unseen genitals, hidden under sagging layers of fat.

"The tattooed faithful," he announces, his voice gurgling and wet like he's got a jarful of honey stuck in his throat. "By my balls, this is our lucky day." The men who set up the table stand at a respectful distance holding their rifles, their eyes dull, faces expressionless.

He walks the line of prisoners, examining us with the penetrating stare of the truly mad. When he notices the branded words on Donovan's forehead, he freezes, his jaw dropping open, eyes widening.

"The branded one," he gurgles. He looks Donovan up and down, marveling over him, gloating over his unexpected prize. "Prayer fucking Donovan. Well, this day just keeps getting better and better." He bows, then makes a flourish with his hand. "Welcome, Prayer, to my traveling carnival of earthly delights."

I lower my head and stare at the ground, hoping in vain he doesn't recognize me.

"And who do we have here?" Valdeez asks, and I know he's talking about me.

"Let me see your face," he commands.

I lift my head. He leans over me, a mountain of heaving skin folds, so close that sweat dropping from his chin falls inches in front of my face.

For a moment he looks confused, his brow rings arranging themselves in furrowed rows. Then he nods, one side of his mouth lifting into a wry smile.

"Indigo Cruz," he snorts. "Now when did you start keeping such enlightened company?"

"I gave my soul to Jesus," I answer, "can't you see the divine joy in my face?"

He erupts into a wheezing fit of laughter. The chain connecting his navel to his cock jangles close to my face.

Valdeez collects himself, crosses his arms. "That'll be the day, Trader Cruz."

He looks down the line of Fundie soldiers, squints in concentration. Behind his bloodshot eyes wheels are turning, questions are being asked. Even with a hash cloud blanketing his mind, Valdeez has one of the sharpest wits around. Crazy as a rabid, starving coyote, for sure, but sharp nonetheless.

"Forced into servitude, I take it?" he asks me. "As a scout, maybe? As a guide for those unfamiliar with these parts?" His eyes burn with intense curiosity. And behind those eyes I sense opportunity, a chance to bargain my way out of here.

I've traded with Valdeez a handful of times over the years, but only when I had to, only when a dry spell had me at the brink of starvation and there was nowhere else to turn. It was tense, dicey business, dealing with the perpetually stoned, always unpredictable Valdeez. After every chancy trade with him, I made the trek back to my turf, half-amazed I'd survived the ordeal, telling myself never again.

He lifts the hairless ridge of pierced skin where his eyebrows used to be. "Don't hold out on me now. And don't mistake this as a negotiation, trader. There's no angle here for you. No cards for you to play. Just my questions and your answers, end of story."

So much for cutting a deal, I guess. "I'm their guide," I admit.

"Guide to where?" he asks.

"Greenies," Donovan mutters, a one-word threat just loud enough so I can hear, reminding me about the card the Fundies still have in the game.

"Guide to where?" Valdeez insists.

Shit! I don't answer.

Enraged, Valdeez reaches out and grabs a handful of Donovan's hair. "What's the game, branded one?" He yanks the Fundie's head back and forth as if he's trying to jar the answer loose. "Where was this trader taking you?"

When Donovan doesn't react or answer, Valdeez lets go and waddles over to Nipple Rings. He reaches out and grasps the chain that connects the man's chest piercings. The soldier glances down, then turns his face away, clenching his jaw in anticipation. Valdeez yanks the chain downward, ripping the rings from the man's chest. Nipple Rings howls in agony and falls forward.

Valdeez tosses the chain over his shoulder and shouts over the cries of the injured man. "Patience is not a virtue your god has seen fit to bless me with, Prayer Donovan."

Then he looks up and down the line of prisoners. "Do

you all know who I am?" he booms as Nipples Rings moans and writhes on the ground. "I had a territory once, east of here. I called it my own turf for the better part of twenty years, where my people ate and drank and traded and screwed and smoked hash. And we minded our own business, never bothering anyone who didn't want to be bothered."

Except when they raided unprotected towns and camps, sportkilling or kidnapping new fuck slaves for their stock. And that wasn't the worst they were known to do. Not by far.

"And then one day," Valdeez continues, glaring at Zara, "these tattooed sons of bitches start showing up, saying they were doing *the Lord's work*. Telling my people to repent, and then pumping them full of buckshot if they didn't."

He pauses in front of Remi, leans down so close their faces nearly touch. Remi squeezes his eyes shut, his chin puckered and trembling. "Now that wasn't exactly the Christian charity my mama told me about, was it?" Valdeez sneers.

"Twenty plus years I held that turf," he repeats, straightening up again, "until these self-righteous devils ran us out. Now we have no turf, no home to call our own. Now we have to wander the wastelands like a pack of feral hounds, living on scraps and leftovers."

The substance of Valdeez's tirade is news to me, though it's hardly a surprise. His territory runs—or ran— alongside the southern end of the Sabine River. It was only a matter of time before Fundie northward expansion knocked on his front door and asked him to get saved or pack his bags. They talked about it sometimes on the trade channels. Toothless Jackson, whose territory near Longview was the closest to Valdeez's turf, figured the bloated hasher and his stoned entourage had at least a few more years before push came to shove, but so much for his expert opinion.

Valdeez steps backwards, his scabby, pockmarked legs a pair of sunburned tree trunks. He grins and moves his eyes down the line of us. "Oh, my lovely Fundie beasties. It's time to pay for your sins." His voice gurgles and sputters. "God indeed is good," he mocks, motioning at one of the guards, who then hurries away and disappears inside the trailer with the smokestack.

Moments after the guard closes the door behind him, someone howls from inside the trailer. It's the girl Miriam. "Stop, please, stop!" she shrieks.

Zara jumps to her feet and the guard nearest to her lunges forward and strikes her hard in the gut with the butt of his rifle. She crumples to the ground, curled up and writhing in the grass, her mouth gulping convulsively as she tries to regain her breath.

Then as suddenly as it started, Miriam's wailing stops.

I picture what's happening inside those metal walls; a cold sweat breaks out on my forehead.

"Temple," I blurt out. "That's where they're headed."

Valdeez pads over to me, gives me a doubtful look. "Temple, you say?"

I nod.

"What the hell's in Temple?" he spits.

I feel the heat of Donovan's eyes on me. "I don't know."

"How's that?" he asks.

"They just told me the where. They didn't tell me the what or why."

Valdeez mulls over my words, staring at me with empty, soulless eyes. Rumbling noises come from inside the trailer.

He turns to Donovan. "What's in Temple, Fundie? What's your mission?"

Donovan says nothing.

Valdeez bends forward, his nose almost touching Donovan's. He lingers there, peering into the branded one's eyes. Donovan doesn't move, doesn't blink.

"I'm not going to waste my time trying to break the great Prayer Donovan," Valdeez says. "One of your people will give it up soon enough."

He straightens back up, grins. "But maybe I'll take a piss on you just for fun, how does that sound?" He bends awkwardly to one side, the belly chain jangling as he reaches down and searches for his cock under folds of skin.

"There we go," he grunts, apparently finding what he was looking for. From the trailer there's a series of loud knocks and the doors creak open. Valdeez drops his cock and looks over. Smoke wafts up from the opening and a shirtless, bony-chested old man appears at the top of the ramp, holding a large round serving tray.

Valdeez claps his hands and rubs them together, visibly pleased. He turns back to Donovan and says, "I'll give you your shower after dinner, branded one."

The old man hunches over the heavy tray, carefully makes his way down the ramp.

As I make out what's on top of the tray, everything around me disappears, falling away in a rush of horrible recognition.

CHAPTER 8

The only sound in the universe is the heavy pulse of my own heartbeat, throbbing in my neck and ears. It's like I'm in a tunnel, silent and airless, and at the end is an image of the tray, the old man's gnarled hands clutching either side as he holds Valdeez's gruesome meal.

A human leg, freshly severed at the knee. Miriam's. Somewhere a woman screams *no no no*. Zara. In my stupor, her wails sound muffled and far away.

The old man places the tray atop the dining table where Valdeez is already seated, sharpening a carving knife as long as his forearm.

"Course one is virgin Fundie tartare," he announces. "A delicacy I've never tried before." He grasps the ankle firmly and plunges the knife into the calf muscle, slicing off a large piece of meat.

I look over at Zara. She's gone berserk. Two of Valdeez's men struggle to hold her down as she shouts the nonsense babble Fundies call speaking in tongues. "HASSANDA BOSSONDA ELAPTEETEE!" She shrieks the phrase over and over at the sky, pleading with a god who isn't listening and isn't there. The veins in her throat bulge and foamy spit leaks from both sides of her mouth.

Nipple Rings retches, a stream of vomit bursting from his mouth and splashing on the ground in front of him.

Next to me, Donovan hasn't moved.

In the corner of my eye I catch Valdeez stabbing the sliced meat with a fork and lifting it to his mouth. I quickly cast my eyes to the ground before I see more.

"Course two will be Fundie ham grilled over mesquite wood," Valdeez announces. "How's it coming along, Cookie?"

"Fine," the old man creaks. "Just fine. About twenty more minutes." I keep my eyes down.

The trailer doors screech open again and I instinctively look over. A tall, muscular man wearing a bloodstained smock stands at the top of the ramp. He holds a cleaver in one hand, and over his opposite shoulder he carries Miriam, her thighs dangling down, the bottom halves of her legs missing. Cloth bandages splotched with blood cover the wounds, bound tightly with rubber tube tourniquets just above the knees.

He strides over, expressionless, and tosses her onto the grass in front of us. The Fundies erupt into a fit of shouts and incoherent raving. Someone grabs me from behind and puts me in a choke hold, pressing their forearm hard against my throat. I flail and try to get out of it, but the hold's in too deep, the arms are too strong. As I struggle in vain, I get a glimpse of the same thing happening down the line, huge men expertly holding each of the prisoners in place. Arms wrapped around necks, knees pressed firmly against backs. Zara, raging with madness, nearly breaks free of the two men trying to contain her when a third arrives and shoves her forward with a boot kick to the shoulder. He then binds her feet as the other two sit on her back and press her face against the ground.

"Can you put them back on? Can somebody put my legs back on?"

In front of me, Miriam has pulled herself up onto her

hands, her half-legs dragging behind. She's heavily drugged, her eyes rolling around crazy and unfocused, her chin shiny with spit. She blathers at Donovan, her speech barely understandable.

"Brother Prayer, can you lay hands on my legs?" she slurs. "Can you heal me?"

Donovan's also immobilized by a choke hold, held by a man even larger than he is. He grits his teeth and stares at the girl.

A round of gunfire explodes into the air, silencing everyone. Standing next to the table, one of Valdeez's lackeys holds a rifle skyward, its barrel still smoking.

"As I was saying," Valdeez says, chewing, "before I was rudely interrupted, the second course will be mesquite-grilled Fundie."

Valdeez stares at Donovan. "And for the third course, I'll carve out her liver while she spends her final moments on this earth watching me enjoy it."

Then he lifts his brows. "Unless you tell me your mission, that is. Then I might find my appetite reduced. Maybe I'll stop at two courses."

I gasp for air, the sweaty arm tight around my neck like a constrictor snake.

The moment stretches on. Finally, Donovan nods.

"Excellent," Valdeez says, clanking his fork down on the plate. He wipes his mouth with a napkin and gets up from the table. He approaches Donovan; the chain from his belly ring hangs low between his legs and clinks with each step.

He stops a few feet in front of the Fundie soldier, blood dripping from the tip of the carving knife still in his hand, and takes a tentative look at the man holding Donovan.

"I've got him," the man assures him, tightening his grip.

Valdeez then gazes down at Donovan. "What's your mission, branded one?"

When Donovan doesn't answer, the large man snorts in frustration. He shakes the knife at Donovan. "What errand has that preacher man sent you on?"

The following seconds are a blur of movements. Donovan twists his body and strikes the man holding him under the chin with a powerful upward blow of his head; his captor releases his grip, groaning and falling backwards like a boxer caught by an unseen punch. In the next instant Donovan's lunging forward, and before Valdeez or anyone else can react, the Fundie soldier's reaching between the giant man's knees, grabbing the cock-end of the chain and yanking it downward in a quick, powerful motion. Valdeez howls and stumbles backwards, dropping the knife and clutching his hands to his groin. He crashes into the dining table, sending plates and glasses and the serving tray flying.

The next thing I know I'm shoved facedown in the dirt, screaming and gunfire exploding all around me. I stay down, flattening my body against the earth as bullets whiz through the air. Men and women yell frantically, their shouts nearly drowned out by the TAT-TAT-TAT of automatic weapons.

"I'm hit, I'm hit!" someone nearby cries.

"Get down! Down!" another voice shrieks.

My cheek pressed to the ground, I feel the vibration of running footsteps all around me. I suddenly realize my eyes are squeezed shut.

Move, Indigo.

Flinching with each burst of gunfire, I lift my head as little as possible and glance around. Bodies strewn across the grass, dead or mostly so. Nipple Rings huddles behind a support leg of one of the trailers, reloading a rifle he must have pulled off one of Valdeez's soldiers. With streaks of blood running down from his chest wounds, he pops in a magazine with the heel of his hand, then aims and fires. Bullets ping and thud against the trailer's steel panels, adding pockmarks to the dented, rust-covered surface.

My wits come back enough for me to realize I'm lying out in the open, in the middle of the crossfire. I ready myself to get up and run, summoning courage or stupidity or whatever else will get my legs to sprint for cover.

One...two...

A hand grabs my upper arm and yanks me up off the ground. I flail about as the hand drags me across the grass. The sudden pressure on my arm is intense and painful, as if it might pop out of the socket from the strain. I twist around and see Donovan, ducking down low as he pulls me toward a trailer with one hand and fires shots from a pistol with the other. I manage to get my legs under me and scramble the rest of the way to the trailer, where Donovan shoves me up the ramp and inside.

"Stay in there," he shouts, then slams the door shut.

I'm plunged into darkness as the gunfire and shouting continues outside. Bullets strike against the outside of the trailer's steel walls; I flinch with each ping. I'm suddenly, sickly aware of the dense aroma of mesquite smoke, of cooking meat, and at the far end there's a soft orange glow of light near the floor. As my eyes adjust, I realize the light's coming from a wood tray for a large square cooker shoved against the back wall. I turn away.

I squat down near the door, my back to the horror behind me, listening to the sounds outside. A chaos of frantic voices and gunfire. The fighting stretches on for what feels like a long time, and then the bullet pings slow and eventually stop. After a tense, lingering silence, I hear voices. Calm voices, relieved voices.

One side seems to have won.

I can't make out who's speaking. I don't know if I'm saved or fucked. Sweat drips down from my forehead and stings my eyes as I sit, quiet and waiting, feeling the heat of the smoker against my back. The latch on the door flips up, the door swings open, and light floods the trailer. I squint and ready myself for the worst.

A familiar silhouette comes into focus, backlit by the

late afternoon sun.

"You hurt?" Donovan asks.

I exhale, then stand on weak, still-trembling legs. "I'm fine."

For the first time in my life, I'm relieved to see a Fundie.

*   *   *

Outside I find a mess of carnage. Bodies everywhere, dozens of them, their arms and legs frozen in unnatural positions. As I take it all in, every exaggeration I've ever heard about the Fundie talent for warfare suddenly seems like a ridiculous underestimate. They had to have been outnumbered at least three-to-one.

Valdeez lies a short distance away, his torso covered in bullet wounds. His face is a mask of surprise, open-eyed and staring at the sky, as if even in death he can't believe what's happened.

It looks like only one of Donovan's squad has been lost. The woman with the cross tattoo on her head lies facedown. One of her squad mates kneels behind her, gently murmuring a quiet prayer.

Then I hear someone sobbing behind me. I turn and see the other Fundie loss. Zara sits on the ground, hunched over Miriam's lifeless body, cradling the girl's head in her lap.

"The Lord is my shepherd," she moans, rocking back and forth like a mother with an infant, "I shall not want. He makes me lie down in green pastures." Her voice breaks and falters as she strokes the dead girl's hair. "He leads me beside still waters."

As I'm turning away, Donovan tugs on my arm. "Come with me." My head swimming, I follow, and behind me Zara's weeping prayers continue. "Even though I walk through the valley of the shadow of death, I will fear no evil."

The branded one gathers what's left of his squad. They stand around him, haggard and staring blankly, the surviving seven of a convoy numbering fifteen only a day ago. Remi fidgets next to Donovan, shifting his weight from one foot to the other, his face twisted and pained. Donovan rests his hand on the boy's shoulder.

"What's the driving time to Temple from here?" Donovan asks me.

"Four or five hours," I mumble. A few feet away a pair of naked bodies lie motionless, their faces obscured by thick grass, their legs splayed across the blood-soaked mattress behind them, as if they tried to get up and run but didn't make it more than a step or two.

Donovan speaks calmly, slowly. First we bury our dead, he says, and then we check the vehicles, see which ones are still drivable.

"Remi, go open up that lot," Donovan tells the boy, pointing to the chain-link fence surrounding Valdeez's vehicles. "Gather up any gear we can use and whatever fuel they got lying around and bring it back here. If any of those vehicles are in good shape, we may want to take 'em." He doles out more orders, sending soldiers off with instructions, telling them to hurry, that there's no time to waste.

When everyone's engaged with their duties, Donovan approaches Zara. She's still clutching the girl's body, singing softly to her. He kneels down next to her and says something I can't make out. Words of comfort, from his tone. He reaches out, touches her shoulder, and Zara erupts, slapping his hand away.

"Don't you touch me!" she yells. "I saw you save that infidel!" She clutches the girl's head protectively. "You could've pulled my girl out of the line of fire, but you saved that trader whore!"

Donovan doesn't react. Zara hunches over the girl and sobs. "Oh, my girl, my sweet, sweet girl."

Donovan kneels there for another minute, then gently

pries Zara's hands from the girl's body. He says something to her and she nods, her arms hanging at her sides and head down, as if all her energy's been expended in grief.

I catch bits and pieces. He's saying something about Miriam going to her reward, his voice calm and reassuring. The reverend's counting on us, he adds.

"We're leaving for Temple in an hour," he says. "I need your help to get us ready."

"Yes, brother," Zara croaks. She wipes her eyes, clears her throat. Donovan helps her to her feet. She gazes down at the girl for a long moment, biting her lip and shaking her head. Then she turns and heads slowly toward the vehicle lot.

It takes a moment for what he's just told her to sink in. *Leaving for Temple?* I startle out of my stupor as if I've been slapped.

I follow Donovan up the ramp of the trailer parked beyond the one with the smokestack. Inside there's a jumbled mess of electronic gear arranged in piles, most of it radio components: mics, antennas, tuners, transceivers, speakers, handheld units. It all looks ancient, even by wastelander standards, the kind of gear that was already outdated before Secession. None of it appears in working order or like it has any hope of ever getting that way. Donovan kneels and starts rummaging, looking for anything he might be able to salvage.

"You can't be serious about Temple," I say.

He ignores me, tosses aside an old CB radio.

I step forward. "You've got what, *half* the squad you started with. And you want to go on?"

He pivots to another pile of useless junk. "You're blocking my light," he grunts. I stay put, furious. What the hell is wrong with these people, with this man?

"If you want to go ahead with this suicide mission, fine," I growl, "but you can find some other idiot to take you there. I'm done." Whatever kept the filter in place between my thoughts and words—fear, caginess, a survival instinct—isn't there any longer.

He stops searching through the gear, wipes his hands on his pants, then stands up. "The hell you are." His face is a cold stone.

"What are you going to do, drag me kicking and screaming?"

"If need be."

I shrug. "Go ahead. Hold a gun to my head. See if it makes a difference."

He studies my face for a moment, then unhooks a water bottle from his belt and holds it out to me. "Take a drink." When I don't move, he adds, "Go on."

I hadn't realized how thirsty I was, but suddenly I'm aware of my parched throat, my sticky, dry tongue. I grab the bottle, gulp down a long swallow, then another.

"So much death and killing," he says, letting out a tired breath. "It ain't an easy thing to shake after."

He notices me clenching and unclenching my fist, trying to get my hand to stop trembling. "Ain't never seen it like this before, have you?" he asks.

I've seen more death than most, I suppose. Bodies left to rot in the desert, whole families hanging from trees. I've seen a man beaten to death in the market for looking at another man's woman. I've seen the ugliest part of human nature expressed a thousand different ways. Birds fly, fish swim, people murder. But I've never seen so much all at once, and never with me in the middle of it.

I hand the water bottle back to Donovan. He hooks it back onto his belt. "We ain't turning back, trader."

I'm about to snap back at him, but the words stick in my throat as something catches my eye on the floor next to his boot. It's a small microphone that's a match for my radio. I quickly look back up and try to push the surprise out of my face.

"It's a fool's errand," I insist. "Can't you see that? Look around here. Luck's not with us on this thing, Fundie. And your god sure as shit isn't lifting a finger to help us."

He stares at me, his gaze suddenly hard and menacing. "Temple ain't that far, trader. It might take me a couple hours longer, but if need be, I can find my way there without no guide."

He rests his hand atop the butt of his holstered pistol. I stand there, stunned by the sudden threat. *Don't forget who you're dealing with, Indigo. Prayer Donovan's a soldier, a killer. He'll send you straight to hell without a second thought if he thinks you're a risk to his holy cause.*

Donovan kneels back down and goes back to rummaging. When his back turns to me, I snatch the microphone off the floor and shove it into my pants pocket.

He examines a receiver, tosses it aside, and sighs. "Ain't nothing here worth taking." Then he stands up. "Come on, we're leaving."

CHAPTER 9

It's late afternoon, and the sun glares at us through the Humvee's front windshield as we head west. I sit in the passenger's seat as Donovan drives, the radio on my lap, the microphone still hidden in my pocket. Ahead, a line of seven trucks stretches a mile in front of us, rolling at a steady pace over the undulating terrain, navigating through or around clusters of mesquite and pecan trees and live oaks. It's spring in Central Texas and the countryside's blanketed with wildflowers. Miles of hills carpeted with the vibrant crimson of Indian paintbrush and the deep magenta of bluebonnets. The kind of impossibly beautiful landscape a painter would have a hard time accurately rendering, a universe away from the horror we've left behind.

Temple is two hours away.

We drive on. The Humvee rocks back and forth as the sun transforms into swollen orange that no longer glares, slowly slipping downward to the horizon.

Nothing will ever be the same. The thought pops into my head out of nowhere as I stare out at the passing fields and trees. For twenty years, I've had a decent run. I carved out a fair-sized trade turf, built a reputation, made some money. I went from a barefoot girl—alone and starving, begging or stealing in the markets—to a woman running the biggest merchant operation east of the Big Empty, with thirty-seven greenies and runners and under-traders working the trade routes in all directions. And if anyone ever gave them shit, all they had to do was say who their patron was, and that was that. Instant respect.

But those days suddenly feel as if they're already fading into the past, as if they were part of someone else's life. Even if I make it out of this alive, even if I make it back home with the greenies, the way of things I've known for the better part of two decades feels as if it's coming to an end. Maybe it has already.

The world's turning upside down. The Fundies continue to expand their turf, and Guzmán's rebellion continues to take city after city, marching ever eastward, the Dallasites unable to stop him. Maybe they can't stop him, and maybe they can't stop Wright, either. More and more lately on the trade channels, there's talk that the Dallasites have grown too soft, safe and secure in their rich, glittering, heavily defended city. Maybe that's why they haven't taken out Guzmán. Maybe that's why they've let Reverend Wright's movement grow out of control. Whatever the reason, the choke hold they've held on the Republic for generations seems to be coming to an end.

A war is coming. An all-out, winner-take-all kind of war. It seems plain now, unavoidable.

I shift my thoughts toward my turf, trying to picture what's going on there right now. Have they started to wonder why I've been gone so long, why I didn't come back in a few hours like I'd said? Are some of them already assuming I'm dead, packing their bags to head out and try their luck on another trader's turf? It doesn't take long for someone to lose faith, assuming they ever had it much of it in the first place.

Time passes and daylight begins to fade as dusk settles over the convoy. With each passing mile, I grow more and more surly, more pissed off at my situation, at the grim prospects waiting for me if I manage to live past Temple.

"He's no saint, your reverend," I grumble. "You know that, right?"

Donovan ignores me.

"All those bribes and corruption with the Dallasites. How do you square that circle, huh? Your holy man with such an unholy alliance?"

The branded one shrugs. "Gotta feed your people somehow."

"And he doesn't give a damn about any refugee children."

No reaction.

"It's a land grab. A power play. That's all this is about, period, end of story." After his threat to send me to hell, I'm probably pushing my luck, but part of me has moved beyond caring.

I let out a hot breath. "You're a bullet in his gun, nothing more. He's got you all so suckered, so taken in with all his holy bullshit. You'd lay down your life for him, kill for him, without so much as a thought. Cannon fodder, every last one of you."

Again, no reaction. Not even a flicker of anger in his expression. After a moment passes, Donovan asks, "You got family, trader?"

"No."

"I did," he says. "Back in Sealy. Five brothers and a sister, all younger than me."

The bottom edge of the sun kisses the horizon. "I don't remember that much about 'em except playing in the woods, catfishing down at the pond." He pauses, then says, "Lost 'em all the day I turned ten, when that monster out of San Antonio and his men showed up."

His words click something in my memory. Old stories about a horde of madmen who torched every town between San Antonio and Houston, killing everyone in their path, burning every building to the ground, leaving nothing but ashes and corpses in their wake. They were led by some blood-hungry psycho. It takes me a moment to remember the name. The Butcher of Bexar County.

"We were down at the pond when it started," Donovan says, his voice low. "We heard the shooting, the screaming. I tried to get the young'uns to hide in the bushes, but they wouldn't have none of it. Stood there crying and hollering for their mamas." He inhales through his nose, slowly lets out the breath from his mouth. "Didn't take 'em long to find us."

Outside, darkness begins to set in. Trees and shrubs take on a hazy, dreamlike quality.

"They shot 'em one after the other, laughing while they did it." He shakes his head. "Little kids who ain't never done nothing to no one."

Donovan clears his throat. "Right as they was turning the gun on me, the reverend came busting out of the woods with a hundred men. Killed every last one of them demons."

The rest of the legend pops into my head: how the crazies never made it to Houston; how Reverend Wright, then a young man, rounded up his small flock of followers and stopped them in a bloody battle at Sealy. *Wright's Sealy Stand.* That was what they called it. The incident that put the reverend on the map; the foundation his reputation as a fearless crusader was built upon.

"When it was all over, I watched him weep over my sister and brothers, trader. Over my parents too. Watched him weep over all them lost children. He picked me up in his arms and carried me out of there."

A long silence follows. One by one, the trucks ahead of us turn on their fog lights. They glow soft and yellow, moving across the darkening hills like pairs of fireflies.

The tragedy of Donovan's family, of his rescue at the hands of Wright, tells me a lot about the man, about his devotion to his cause. But it's a story that's no worse than a million other stories in this cursed land, mine included.

And it's far from the worst I've ever heard.

Of all the human weaknesses I've seen in my time—greed, lust, stupidity, arrogance—faith has to be the worst of them all. Faith in people, faith in some invisible man, faith in anything. Faith can get you killed, especially the blind type, the variety Donovan practices.

A few miles ahead a scattering of electric lights spread across a wide, flat plain.

Temple.

CHAPTER 10

We hide in a dense grove of oak trees, waiting for Donovan's return. Behind us the trucks are covered in branches and underbrush, hurriedly camouflaged by the squad as Donovan left with Remi on foot to recon the Unaffil's fleet. A full moon illuminates our surroundings with a pale, ghostly light. Crickets chirp in rhythm, their high-pitched squeak the only sound in the chilled evening air. We lie on our bellies atop a small rise, watching and waiting. A few miles below us, Temple bustles with an unusual amount of activity. Normally a sleepy, mostly deserted town of crumbled buildings and few residents, its streets now teem with hundreds of people, maybe thousands. Wires hung with electric lights crisscross the streets, brought to shining life by portable generators. Barrel fires glow and flicker throughout the city, each surrounded by small crowds like fluttering moths.

"So many of them," Nipple Rings whispers. "There's so many."

And so few of us.

"We've got the Lord on our side," Zara answers, predictably.

The girl Miriam had Him on her side, too, didn't she?

All the good it did her.

We wait there for over an hour. Finally two shadows approach, hunched over and jogging. Donovan shoulders his way through the wall of brush into our hiding place, Remi following behind. Every pair of eyes fixes on the branded one, waiting for him to speak.

"You see it?" Zara asks, her voice tight, anxious. "You see the fleet?"

Donovan looks at her, nods. "They're still using the airstrips at the army base." He takes out a hunting knife and kneels to draw shapes in the dirt with one hand, holding a small flashlight with the other. "Ten rows of vehicles, lined up nice and neat." He scratches long lines in the dirt, points his finger between them. "We can lay the charges here, here, and here."

He looks up at Zara. "Close to a thousand trucks and cars down there. We got enough to get 'em all?"

Zara furrows her brow, staring at the scratches in the dirt as she works out an answer. After a moment, she nods. "We space it out right, oughta be enough."

"It don't have to be perfect," Donovan tells her. "They ain't gonna go on no raid if we leave 'em with fifty trucks. We just gotta get most of them."

For a while they murmur back and forth, planning their approach, deciding who'll go where and who'll do what while Zara lays the charges. It's hard to follow. The conversation is layered with phrases and words my trader's ears don't recognize, a kind of soldier's shorthand. Maneuvers and battle tactics. It might as well be in Chinese. Nipple Rings and another soldier remove the covering of brush from two of the Humvees, the ones carrying the explosives. Both trucks have small motorbikes attached to racks on their rear hatches.

When they start the engines, the rest of the squad piles into the two trucks. Donovan turns to me. "Stay here, stay hidden." Then he hands me a set of keys and nods at one of the trucks. "For the Chevy over there." I grip the key in my hand. Cold metal against my sweaty palm. I stare at it dumbly, not quite believing he just gave me a ticket out of here.

"Ain't nothing to prevent you from taking off on us," he says, as if he knows what I'm thinking, "but you'd be better off with an escort to get you back safe."

I nod. "I understand. I'll wait." Total lie.

Donovan nods, but his eyes are skeptical. He's not convinced I'll stick around, but he's not going to waste time discussing it. He's got bigger things to worry about. "If we ain't back in a couple hours, we probably ain't coming back. You get on out of here, you hear me?"

"Got it."

There's a moment of awkwardness. Under other circumstances I might say good luck or he might say stay safe, but this isn't one of those times or places. He nods at me, turns, and climbs into the lead Humvee. The pair of trucks slowly exits the clump of trees, their lights off, sticks and dry leaves crunching under their tires. I watch them pull away, box-shaped silhouettes dissolving into the darkness, the low rumble of engines fading. Another minute and they're gone.

And then I'm alone.

*　　*　　*

My hands shaking with excitement, I start the Chevy's motor, then watch as the fuel needle floats slowly to the right. A full tank. Okay, I'm out of here.

I reach for the shifter and put it into drive, but then I pause a moment, pondering my next move. Moments earlier, when I'd watched the squad disappear into the night, my first instinct was to drive east, to put as much distance between myself and whatever hell's about to break out in Temple. But then after that, what?

Going back for the greenies on my own won't work. If I were to show up in Wright's camp without Donovan's squad, there would be tons of questions. Where are the soldiers? What happened in Temple? Was the mission successful? Questions I wouldn't be able to answer. And God knows where things would go from there. Nowhere good, that's for damn sure. They certainly wouldn't send us all on our way with a handshake and a smile. The more I turn it over in my mind, the more obvious the answer becomes. The only way they make it out of there alive is if I come back with the soldiers, which means I have to wait here for their return.

Save yourself, Indigo. There's nothing you can do for them. I could start a new turf, maybe somewhere up near Texarkana, far away from all this mess. I tell myself this over and over, trying not to picture Jak and Shooter's faces, twisted with worry. Trying not to wonder, morbidly curious, how long it'll take all of them to lose hope, to realize that I'm never coming for them.

"Goddammit!" I shout, slamming the shifter back into park. I pound my fist against the steering wheel.

One hour, I decide, my hand throbbing. That's all I'm going to give them to get back here. Not a minute more.

*　　*　　*

Some time later, I nod off, startle awake, then drift off again. Alone in the dark, everything around me quiet and still, I'm overcome with a sudden tiredness. I bite the inside of my mouth, pinch my thighs until I wince to keep myself awake.

Minutes creep by. I don't have a clock on me, and the one in the Humvee's dashboard doesn't work. I'm not sure how much time has passed. Thirty minutes? Forty-five?

I squint through a gap in the branches, searching in the direction the squad headed. There's nothing but empty darkness.

Then I see something. Lights. They look like flickering flashlights, I think at first, the sudden, faraway flashes. But a moment later the sound reaches me—the popping of automatic weapons—and my stomach twists in panic. A second later the night explodes into a fireworks show of muzzle flashes and tracers zipping across the dark landscape.

So much for your covert operation. Time to get out of here.

I turn the ignition, rev the engine, slam the stick into drive. Tree branches snap and crack as I push the truck through a wall of low-hanging limbs. I turn the wheel over, whipping the truck around, away from the firefight.

Then my foot reflexively hits the brake, jerking the truck to a stop. Ahead of me, four pairs of headlights bear down on my location, growing steadily brighter. *What the hell?* Before I can even think if they've seen me or not, there's a loud, crunching POP and a large spiderweb crack bursts across my windshield.

Shit!

I stomp on the gas, spinning the truck around in the opposite direction. The tires slide in the dirt, then gain traction, and the Chevy lurches forward. A few seconds later I'm barreling over an unseen landscape at a dangerous, risky speed. If I hit a ditch at the wrong angle or run over a tree stump, I'm screwed. Bullets ping and ricochet, hammering the truck. I hunch low over the wheel, trying to keep my head down. Straight ahead the gunfight continues, getting closer and louder. I spot the two Humvees the squad left in, and as they grow larger in my headlights, I see they're empty of soldiers. Then the thought strikes me that the vehicles may still be loaded with explosives.

I take a hard left, steering the truck away from the Humvees. The Chevy tips sickeningly as both wheels on the left side lift off the ground. My body stiffens with a here-we-go feeling, but the truck doesn't roll. Instead, the vehicle falls back onto four wheels and there's a violent CLANK from the undercarriage. Metal grinds against metal beneath my feet, the sound of things tearing apart.

Something big and important, probably an axle, has broken. Momentum carries the truck forward a few more yards before it comes to a complete stop. The motor sputters and dies.

Panic seizes me. I look toward the chase group. They're farther away than before, wisely choosing not to match my reckless speed, but closing fast. I have no weapons, no radio, and except for a container of fuel in the bed, the truck's empty. I kill the Chevy's lights and get out. Bursts of automatic gunfire crackle, glowing tracers zip back and forth.

For a moment I freeze, not knowing which way to run. Then I see them. The Fundie squad, hunkered down behind a clump of trees. Glimpses of soldiers shooting at an unseen enemy, their prone figures flat against the ground, illuminated by the flare of their firing weapons. In the darkness it's hard to tell how far away they are. A hundred yards? More?

A volley of bullets thud-thud-thuds the dead truck's body. I scramble away from the vehicle and sprint toward the squad. I don't look back as I half-run, half-stumble forward in the dark over rough, bumpy ground. As I approach, I wave my arms frantically and scream my name, expecting a bullet to take me down at any moment.

Then Donovan's there, the top half of his torso appearing from behind a tree, barely visible in the darkness. He's gesturing at me, waving me forward.

"Get in here!" he shouts.

I keep low, running past him and into the thicket as he shoulders his rifle and fires at my pursuers.

"Stay down," he barks, but I'm already flat on my stomach. My heart feels like a hammer beating against the inside of my chest. Ahead of me, his squad squeezes off short bursts of gunfire, peering into the blackness with night vision specs. Nipple Rings looks back at me and shouts, "Welcome to the party, trader!" Zara turns and scowls at me, then turns back and fires her weapon.

Behind us, Donovan's shots seem to have taken the chase group by surprise. The headlights break formation, scattering apart. A moment later they're heading away, red taillights bouncing up and down as they make their retreat.

Donovan kneels next to me. "You hit?"

I shake my head. "No. What happened?"

"We got the charges laid out," he tells me. Over our heads bullets rip through the thick canopy of leaves. "But they spotted us before we could detonate and opened up on us. We had to fall back."

He orders me to keep my head down, then crawls over next to Zara.

I lie there frozen, watching them. Zara shouts something to Donovan, pointing repeatedly in the direction of the gunfire. He shakes his head, shouts back. I wiggle forward, moving closer to them. Remi lies on his side, expertly reloading pistols and rifles. He nods at me as I crawl past.

"We can't leave the job undone!" Zara's yelling, her face inches from Donovan's. "Reverend's counting on us!"

Donovan shouts, "Incoming fire's too heavy. We gotta find a way around."

"There ain't no time to go around!" Zara cries back. "How long you think till the rest of the town's up here? How long you think till they find them charges?"

I look back at Remi. He's no longer loading weapons. Suddenly he's listening intensely to Donovan and Zara.

My pulse races, my mind whirs. Beyond our hiding place in the trees, some fifty yards away, one of the Humvees sits, riddled with bullets. The other one is maybe another fifty yards beyond it, a dark outline against the yellow city lights in the distance.

Bullets slice through tree branches. Bark and wood explode into splinters and rain down on our heads. The rate of fire increases, and a raw panic begins to spread through my body. I press my body to the dirt. Nipple Rings and his squad mates return fire.

"There's more coming!" Zara shouts. "We can't wait! We gotta set 'em off!"

Zara peers over at Remi. "We gotta set 'em off," she repeats, addressing only to the boy this time. Remi stops loading the weapon and his eyes lock with Zara's. They share a meaningful look, some unspoken message passing between them. A moment passes, then Remi nods.

"Bless you, child," Zara cries. Remi springs to his feet and bolts out of the thicket.

"Where you going, boy? Get back here," Donovan shouts. He rises up, but Zara throws herself at him, knocking him to the ground.

I lift my head, and through a gap in the bushes I see Remi sprinting for the Humvee.

"What's he doing?" someone shouts.

Remi reaches the Humvee, bullets pinging against the sheet metal body, sending sparks flying. He unhooks the small motorbike from the back of the vehicle and lowers it to the ground. Then he opens the truck's rear hatch and pulls out something that looks like a piece of heavy clothing. Nipple Rings squeezes off a long volley of covering fire.

Zara struggles to keep Donovan on the ground. "Get off me, woman," he grunts. He pushes her off of him and lifts himself to his knees. She tries to grab him again, but he slaps the side of her head hard. "What in God's name's gotten into you?"

"Suffer little children," Nipple Rings cries, "and forbid them not, to come unto me."

The woman next to him shouts, "For of such is the kingdom of heaven!"

The rest of the squad breaks out in tongues, filling the air with shrieking gibberish and gunfire.

Over at the Humvee, Remi's putting an arm into what appears to be a large vest. He inserts his other arm, then shrugs the garment onto his shoulders. It's ridiculously oversized, hanging low to his knees. He moves stiffly and slowly, as if suddenly burdened with a heavy load.

My throat suddenly constricts as I realize he's wearing a bomb vest, packed with explosives. The boy ties a drawstring around his waist, picks up the motorbike, and throws a leg over the seat.

"Remi," Donovan shouts. "No!" He's already out of the thicket, running toward the boy.

Remi kick-starts the motor and revs the throttle. He looks back at Donovan, holds his hand up for a moment as if to say goodbye, then guns the motors and speeds away before Donovan can reach him.

Donovan stops and watches the boy accelerate into the darkness, then he raises his rifle and lays down a long stream of covering fire. "Remi," he shouts between bursts. "Remi!"

The motorbike disappears into the night, the whine of its motor climbing and dropping as the boy works through the gears. Donovan lays down more covering fire.

"Prayer," Zara calls out. "Get to cover!"

He doesn't listen as he pops a fresh ammo clip into his rifle and continues firing off rounds. Nipple Rings and Zara rush out of the thicket and grab him by the shoulders. He pulls away and elbows Nipple Rings in the face, sending the man to the ground. Zara pleads with him to get out of the open, yanking on his arm, trying to pull him back. "You're gonna get hit out here, Prayer, come on!"

Donovan shoves her away. Nipple Rings gets up and begins to shoot in the same direction as Donovan. More covering fire for the boy Remi. Then Zara raises her rifle and does the same. The rest of the squad comes out of the thicket and joins them. I watch them, a line of soldiers standing shoulder to shoulder, muzzle flares bursting from their weapons.

Then time stops.

A brilliant flash lights up everything around us like a sudden, white sun. An image of Donovan's squad, standing together, silhouetted by the blinding light, sears itself into my eyes. Then the flash winks out, and a shock wave rips through the air and ground, hitting me like some huge invisible fist. My vision shakes chaotically and the deafening roar of an explosion fills my head. It feels as if the entire universe is tearing apart. I'm not sure what's up and what's down or if I'm still on the ground or being tossed through the air.

Then the ground stills itself under my belly, and through the flash spots in my eyes I can see clouds rising in the near distance. Four, five, six of them, glowing orange and rushing up into the sky. The airstrip, I think, imagining hundreds of cars and trucks, charred and burning.

The next thing I know, hands are pulling me up off the ground. I look up and see Zara, pointing and barking orders, but I can't hear her over the ringing of my ears.

Nipple Rings puts his face close to mine, yells something. I stare at him stupidly, too stunned to speak. "Can you walk?" he asks, his eyes large and white. I nod reflexively and he helps me stand.

I stumble through a grassy field on shaky, unsure legs, supported by soldiers holding my upper arms. We steal away across an open plain. The tinny buzz in my ears dies down enough for me to realize we're not being shot at. There's no gunfire, no sound at all except the heavy breathing of the squad and the muffled fall of their footsteps on the soft grass.

"Look," someone whispers. "Over there. Look how the Lord provides for his people."

Two trucks sit side by side, idling in a field with their lights off, both drivers dead. One's hunched over the steering wheel, the other's leaning back against the seat, head up, mouth gaping open.

My swirling mind begins to settle, thoughts slowly gain coherence. The trucks must have been part of the group chasing me. Hit by Donovan's shots when I ran past him into the thicket.

The squad removes the bodies from the vehicles. Soldiers climb into the beds and seconds later we're moving steadily eastward, lights off, rolling away from the burning inferno behind us.

Donovan drives. I sit between him and Zara, sounds and pictures echoing through my mind. The whine of a motorbike's engine, the image of Remi disappearing into the night. I turn and look back. The orange blaze of hundreds of burning vehicles glows in the distance, then disappears as we come around a hill.

No one's firing at us, and there are no vehicles on our tail. I take a long, deep breath as it finally occurs to me that I might actually make it back home alive. But it's difficult to feel relieved as I sit between the two Fundies, difficult to feel anything but the heavy, palpable tension in the darkened truck cab.

"He was doing the Lord's work," Zara mutters after a long silence, her tone defensive.

Donovan doesn't respond. I feel his body tense up beside me.

"He's with Jehovah now," she continues. "Christ has a special place in heaven for martyr children. He takes them into his loving—"

"Don't say another word about that boy, woman," Donovan seethes. He turns, and his moonlit face is a mask of genuine hatred. I want to sink to the floorboard.

"Not another goddamn word," he warns. "Ever."

CHAPTER 11

A few minutes later we come upon the clump of trees where the squad's remaining trucks were hidden. Whether we found the place by sheer luck or sharp eyes, I can't be sure.

"Why are we stopping?" I ask, looking behind us nervously.

Donovan taps the dashboard. "Not enough gas to get back." I look down, see the fuel gauge needle resting atop the E.

The soldiers quickly and quietly uncover their vehicles. Zara exits the passenger door without a word to Donovan. Seconds later we start rolling eastward again, leaving the Unaffils' trucks and their empty tanks behind.

We make our way around the southern tip of Belton Lake, and Donovan pauses the convoy in a shallow valley. The squad organizes itself for the long drive back, distributing hand radios to each driver, divvying up bags of fuel pellets. I stay in the truck alone and watch. It all happens rapidly, efficiently, and with very few words spoken.

When they finish, Donovan slides back into the driver's seat and the truck's engine rumbles to life. Nipple Rings then appears next to the vehicle on Donovan's side. "Brother Prayer," he asks, "should we send somebody back? To check on the job?"

It's hard to imagine a single vehicle surviving the powerful blasts and the ensuing inferno that was visible for miles, but we didn't stick around long enough to make sure. We were too busy scrambling for our lives in the other direction.

Donovan stares straight ahead and doesn't answer. He looks haggard, worn out.

"Brother Prayer?" Nipple Rings asks lightly.

And then I think: *the radio.*

"I can check on the trade channels," I say. "Odds are they're talking about it."

Donovan nods once. "Bring it to her," he tells Nipple Rings.

The soldier returns quickly with the radio and hands it to me. I place it on the seat between me and Donovan. The little unit squeaks and cracks as I power it up and fiddle with the dials, searching for chatter. Nipple Rings stands nearby, watching my fingers work the dials, his expectant gaze glowing in the truck's dome light. The branded one orders the soldier back to his vehicle and soon we're heading out, eastward bound, our returning convoy half its original number.

I listen carefully, hearing lots of chatter. An unusual amount, it seems. Most of it's bullshit, of course, made-up stories and meaningless babble broadcast by under-traders and greenies to throw off any untrained ears who might be listening in. It takes a while to filter through all of it, to find the right frequency. But eventually I get there.

A few words and phrases click in my head and there's a flash of understanding. They're talking about what happened in Temple. I increase the volume a notch.

"You find some—"

I jerk my hand up, showing Donovan my palm to quiet him.

I lean closer over the radio, close my eyes, and let the rushing river of words—that complex, dense, ever-changing language known as traderspeak—flow over me. I begin to pick out meaningful bits and pieces, and a conversation slowly takes shape.

Temple. Total destruction of hundreds of cars and trucks. Dozens killed.

For some time I listen, and it becomes clear I wasn't the only trader who didn't know what the Unaffils were up to. Voices bicker at each other over the airwaves. *How could they stockpile that many vehicles right under your nose and you didn't notice? Don't you have any people planted there?* Then someone else—a voice I think I recognize from Sanchez's turf—answers back defensively. *Who's* ever *put a plant in the Big Empty? Nothing ever happens there.*

They go round and round like that for some time. After a while, I lower the volume. "It's destroyed," I tell Donovan.

"The whole fleet?" he asks.

"Sounds like it. That's all they're talking about. That and kicking themselves for not knowing about it in the first place."

Donovan nods. "Anything else?"

I keep listening, but it's the same thing over and over. They're putting the pieces together over the airwaves, working it all out. They must have been gearing up to raid that relief convoy, says one. Someone else agrees, repeating yes, yes, that has to be it. Never would have guessed those Unaffils would have teamed up like that, a third voice comments. The other two agree.

All this *and* Guzmán to worry about, the first voice adds.

Wait, what? I hear it just as I'm reaching to turn off the radio.

Donovan notices my hand jerk back. "What is it?"

"Not sure," I answer. "Give me a minute."

I close my eyes and concentrate. The voices on the

radio have stopped talking about the raid on Conroe and the huge fleet of smoldering vehicles in Temple. Now they're going on about Guzmán. Where he is now, which direction he's going. My heart starts racing as they go over last known locations and speculate about the number of vehicles. Their voices crack and strain with worry. *What's he after? Why is he doing this? It doesn't make any sense!*

I open my eyes, trying to process what I've just heard.

"Tell me," Donovan says.

I stare at him, my mind still buzzing.

"Spill it, trader," he insists.

"Guzmán's army is on the move," I tell him.

"On the move?" he asks. "Headed where?"

I swallow. "Here."

* * *

If it weren't for bad luck, you'd have no luck at all, Indigo Cruz.

The Humvee's parked on a hilltop, the highest nearby spot where Donovan can get a good view to the west. The squad waits for us down below, still parked in the shallow valley. I sit in the passenger seat, my elbow propped against the door frame, fist to my cheek. The branded one stands on the roof with a pair of binoculars, scanning the westward landscape. With each passing minute, the surrounding countryside becomes clearer in the creeping light of dawn. Haziness recedes, edges sharpen. A light coating of morning fog blankets the low spots between the rolling hills.

I curse myself for being so stupid, for not keeping my mouth shut. *You didn't have to say a thing about that Guzmán business, did you? You could have been on your way back home already. But no, you had to give him something else to worry about, had to open your mouth before your brain kicked in. Idiot.*

On my lap, the radio pops and buzzes as I dial through the channels. I listen, change frequencies, listen again, but there's nothing. There hasn't been any chatter for the last half hour, not since the comments about Guzmán's big push eastward. They didn't go into details, frustrating me almost as much as Donovan. About all I could gather was that a shitload of Guzmán's vehicles are pushing across the plains in a big hurry, and they were last seen near San Angelo, some fifty miles west of where we are right now.

Donovan climbs down off the roof. "Anything?"

I shake my head. "Not a word."

He grunts. "I don't see nothing west of us."

"Maybe he's taking San Angelo," I suggest. It seems the most likely explanation. Guzmán's been ripping town after town out of the Dallasites' tightfisted control out in the western desert, slowly pushing his way east, expanding his territory and getting pretty damned rich in the process. In just a few years, his little rebellion that started with a dozen bandits capturing a natgas processing plant outside of El Paso has grown into a full-fledged revolution, boasting thousands of followers and holding a sizeable chunk of the Republic's natgas supply. San Angelo's the next major town in his path, the next logical target.

"Could be," Donovan replies, scratching his stubble. "But didn't he just take Odessa?"

"Last week," I reply, nodding. It had been all over the trade channels.

He gazes westward and squints, as if Guzmán's plans might be found somewhere on the horizon if he looks hard enough. Then he exhales and shakes his head. "Seems awful quick to take another town. It don't add up."

So let's not try to add it up. "We can't stick around here," I urge him, clicking off the radio.

He spits on the ground. "I reckon not."

Donovan walks around and climbs in the driver's side. He stares down at the dashboard and lets out a long breath. I watch his face for a moment, his tired, deeply lined face. He looks…burdened, as if he's carrying some invisible heaviness. Maybe it's the decades of killing and conquering, of watching his soldiers suffer and die, of seeing unspeakable human horrors, that thing that drove him into retirement and isolation. But then maybe it's not that complicated. Maybe it's just the deaths of the boy Remi and the girl Miriam, the full force of their tragic ends finally hitting him.

"He seemed like a good kid," I say. "I'm sorry."

Donovan nods, keeps gazing downward. He only seems partly present, the better part of his attention lost somewhere deep inside his own thoughts. After a few moments, he lifts his head and looks into the distance. His brow slowly furrows in confusion.

"What do you make of that, trader?" he asks.

I turn and look. About a mile away, close to the lake, there's a sedan—maybe a Lincoln or an Olds—with oversized suspension and huge knobby tires, driving slowly near the lake shore.

Jesus, what now?

"No idea," I answer. There aren't any other vehicles. Whoever it is, they're traveling alone.

"Good Lord," Donovan exclaims. I look at him and he's got the binoculars pressed to his face. "I don't believe it."

*   *   *

Donovan calls the others over his hand radio, and soon we're following the mysterious Lincoln from a safe distance. The convoy creeps along in single file, staying hidden behind trees like a pack of feral dogs patiently stalking their prey.

The travelers park the Lincoln on a hilltop overlooking the lake and get out. Donovan halts the convoy, stretches his hand out the window to make some signal to the squad. The soldiers exit their vehicles. I step out of the passenger side—keenly aware that I'm unarmed—keeping close to Donovan as the squad creeps forward through the dense maze of branches and underbrush.

Donovan stops the squad about twenty meters away from the Lincoln. Through a wall of leaves I can see there are four of them. A young man and woman, a skinny, fiftyish man with blond hair pulled back into a ponytail, and a large, muscled man with close-cropped hair. The muscled man turns to one side and I see breast lumps. Not a man, a woman. A tank of a woman.

The branded one turns to me. "Stay here," he whispers. Then he signals to the squad and they emerge from their hiding places, guns in hand, to confront the travelers.

All the travelers' hands go straight into the air, except those of the tank woman. She crosses her huge arms and scowls at the Fundies. Nipple Rings slowly approaches her and removes her gun belt and the large hunting knife tied to her thigh. Her three companions look terrified, all open-mouthed and wide-eyed, the same expression I'd have if a pack of armed Fundies jumped out of a thicket behind me. The tank woman, amazingly, just looks annoyed.

Then I notice the man with the ponytail has a dog collar around his neck. It's one of those numbers with nanowire inside, torture tech smuggled in from the States or China, the kind of toy Dealer Valdeez might have liked to play with. Somewhere there's a remote control that can tighten the wire from neck-sized to pinky finger-sized in the blink of an eye, killing its wearer instantly in the bloodiest, messiest way imaginable.

I can't make out what they're saying, but there's a bit of talk back and forth, and then a remote appears and the young woman deactivates the collar. The man with the ponytail hesitates for a moment, then carefully removes it, lifting it over his head. Zara takes the collar and tosses it into the brush.

Donovan approaches the tank woman, points to what looks like some kind of pendant hanging from her chest. She grabs his hand and I hear her say *don't touch it* in Spanish. No la toques. Her voice is a low growl.

The Fundie soldiers react by raising their weapons at

the woman, but Donovan waves them off. Then he says something to her, and I catch a tone of familiarity in his voice, like he knows her. She must have been the one he recognized in the binoculars.

"I know who you are," he says. "And I know who you're with now."

They bind the travelers' hands behind their backs and usher them into separate vehicles. Donovan waves me over to the Lincoln, where he's standing on the running board.

"Get in," he barks at me, then climbs into the driver's side.

I go over and open the passenger's side, finding the man with the ponytail sitting in the middle of the front seat. His pale blue eyes are the nervous stare of a frightened animal. Next to him, Donovan turns the ignition and the engine rumbles to life.

"Come on, trader," he calls. I hop in and slam the door shut. A moment later Nipple Rings appears at my window, the shortwave radio in hand.

He passes it to me. "Thanks," I say. He leaves with a nod, and I place the radio on my lap. The man beside me stares at it like it's a plate full of barbecue ribs and he hasn't eaten in days.

Donovan raises a hand radio to his mouth. "We're heading east," he announces to the squad. "They ought to be at Conroe by now. God willing, we'll make it back there before nightfall."

The Fundie soldiers react with shouts and hollers, gunshots firing skyward in celebration as Donovan turns the big sedan eastward.

"Conroe?" I ask Donovan.

He glances at me and nods, but offers no explanation. "Just sit back and relax, trader," Donovan says, maneuvering the vehicle around a ditch.

Either he doesn't want to tell me in front of the ponytailed man, or he doesn't want to tell me at all. I shrug off the question since it hardly matters. Conroe was the reverend's target all along, whether Donovan's mission was a success or not. Wright likely headed there as soon as we left him, anxious to start converting souls as soon as possible.

I'm tired, drained of the strength required to ask more questions, to find out more about Conroe or about our new passengers. All that matters now is that in a handful of hours I'll be home.

CHAPTER 12

We make our way east across the rolling landscape, navigating around enormous groves of oaks and pines—green and dense and impassable—that cover large swaths of the countryside.

I mess around with the radio distractedly, watching the countryside pass by and searching through the channels the way I've done thousands of times: my fingers on autopilot, my ears on auto-listen. There's idle chatter, but it's all nonsense talk, intentional static. Nothing about the fireworks in Temple and no more mention of Guzmán's army. I still have the microphone hidden in my pocket. All I'd need is five minutes of talk time with friendly traders out west to get the latest whats and wheres of Guzmán's rolling army, but Donovan would never risk letting me say a word over the airwaves. Maybe it's better this way, better we don't really know how close they are. The more uncertainty Donovan has, the more likely he'll be to distance himself from the threat, which is my silver lining as it ends up with me getting home quicker.

Miles pass under the Lincoln's tires, and I breathe easier as we put more distance between ourselves and the Big Empty. It's late afternoon; I feel the sun low in the sky behind us, warm on my shoulders and neck. I noodle over what's ahead of us, and I entertain the idea of maybe making some trade arrangement with Wright when we get back. This little mission might have bought me a fair amount of goodwill, and it might not be a bad idea to cash in on it.

My thoughts argue with one another for some time, weighing the good and the bad of getting into bed with Wright. It's a tough call, with no easy answer, and at the end of the day it's as much about survival as it is money. Up in Dallas, the Bullocks and their cronies seem to be weakening by the minute, yielding to Wright's Fundies and letting them take more and more political control in the southeast while they lose towns and natgas fields to Guzmán out west. Dallas is less a capital nowadays than it is a high-tech bunker for the rich, a golden cage protected by airborne drones. And while it's not an all-out war yet between the Guzmán and Fundie and Dallas factions, it feels like that's just around the corner, like everything's close to a breaking point.

War is coming, maybe the kind of war where everyone has to pick a side. Even traders who hate picking sides.

My tired mind wanders and the concentration I need to make sense of the radio chatter fades. The talk over the trade channels becomes a meaningless blur.

Next to me the ponytailed man fidgets and clears his throat, like he's about to speak but then decides against it. He's thin, filthy, and his skin looks like some kind of dried fruit that's been left in the sun too long, all wrinkled and brown and sagging. Was he that tank woman's prisoner? Even through all the tiredness, there's a curiosity I can't entirely shut off. A trader's paranoia, I suppose. Always needing to know who's who and what's what. Never wanting to be out of the know.

"So who was that woman?" I ask Donovan. "You know her?"

Donovan glances at the man between us for a moment,

then turns his eyes forward again and nods.

"From where?" I ask.

"I seen her fight before," he answers.

"Fight?"

"Bare-knuckle bouts out west," Donovan says. "Few years back." He glances again at the ponytailed man. "Before she went to work for Guzmán."

I stiffen at the name. "How do you know she went to work for Guzmán?"

"She never lost a bout. When a fighter like that leaves the game, folks talk about it." He shakes his head. "I seen her KO a man who musta had fifty pounds on her."

I've never followed the fights, so it's no wonder I've never heard of her. Whenever they talked about it on the trade channels, they could go on for hours, recalling the best bouts they ever saw or arguing over who had the best left hook of all-time. Barbaric spectacles aren't my thing, so I never listened or kept up with it.

"She's a tough one," the ponytailed man agrees, the first words he's uttered in hours. "But I ain't with 'em. And I ain't with Guzmán, either. I swear." His voice is jittery and nervous.

"So who *are* you with, then?" I ask.

He shrugs. "Just kinda on my own, I reckon."

"And what is it you were doing, exactly," I prod, "out in the middle of nowhere? Where were you heading?"

He shrugs again.

I sigh. *Leave it alone, Indigo. You're almost home.* Maybe they're scouting for Guzmán, maybe they're deserters from his army. It's not my concern, so I should just enjoy the ride and let the old bugger live with the illusion that he can keep his secrets. He'll find out otherwise soon enough. Wright's soldiers will have him coughing up everything he knows inside of a minute.

Then a scary thought strikes me: what if there's a connection between these travelers and Guzmán's rolling army? What if he's chasing after *these very people we just picked up?*

No, I decide, discarding the idea. It can't be. You don't send an army after four people. Nobody's that valuable. I rub my eyes and tell myself I'm reaching, that my tired mind has come up with a ridiculous possibility. Whatever the tank woman and her fellow travelers are up to or not up to, it's Wright's puzzle to work out, not mine.

Time passes and daylight begins to fade. We rack up the miles steadily, and we make good time as I give Donovan small course adjustments, guiding the convoy's route, keeping us in a beeline for Conroe. About an hour ago we passed College Station, the enormous, crumbling football stadium moving past us on our right-hand side, the last landmark on our return trip. From here it's maybe another couple hours, a straight shot southeast to Lake Conroe, where I gather the reverend and his crew will be waiting for us, no doubt converting scores of new souls to his sacred cause. The starving and desperate are always easy marks; they'll buy just about anything. Empty bellies and troubled minds are a trader's favorite customers. A preacher's too.

The Lincoln jolts to a stop, and I slap my palms on the dashboard to catch myself. The ponytailed man, with his hands tied behind him, slides forward and smashes his chest against the dash. He groans in pain like someone's kicked him in the stomach and slides down to the floorboard. Donovan grabs his upper arm and yanks him back up onto the seat.

"What's going on?" I ask. The old man gulps like a fish, trying to get his breath.

Donovan peers into the rearview. He wheels the vehicle around and approaches the pickup behind us. All the trucks except ours have come to a stop. Nipple Ring's voice crackles from the hand radio. One of his tires has a slow leak.

"I'll give you a hand," Donovan calls back. Then he kills the engine and looks at us. "Don't go nowhere."

Like there's anywhere to go.

As soon as he shuts the door behind him, the ponytailed man starts chattering.

"Y'all taking us to Fundie turf?" he asks.

I don't reply.

"You don't strike me as no Fundie," he says. "I'd say you're a trader by the looks of you. That what you are, a trader?"

I don't say anything, instantly annoyed. He reminds me of a low-rent market hustler, the kind who tries to sell you a bundle of rotten peppers hidden under a thin layer of fresh ones. The kind who grabs your arm and keeps trying to sell you when you turn to walk away. No, that's too generous. His vibe is more like some slimy pimp, jittery and anxious to whore out his boy or girl, insisting you won't find a better piece of ass this side of the Sabine River.

He turns and looks to make sure Donovan is still out of earshot. He speaks low, like all of a sudden we're buddies sharing a secret. "I got information, woman. The kind a smart trader like you would want to know."

It's a blunt, clumsy pitch, but then Donovan will be back in a minute. If he wants me to buy whatever he's selling, he has to act quickly. There's no time for an artful con.

As much as I want to ignore this filthy, toothless bugger, the trader in me begrudgingly decides to listen. The best deals are sometimes the ones you stumble into by accident, the ones that fall out of the sky and land in your lap.

"All right," I exhale tiredly, as if I don't have the least bit of interest, "what do you got?"

He takes another nervous glance back at Donovan, who's already got the tire changed, pumping the jack handle to lower the car back onto four wheels.

"But you gotta let me go," he blathers. "I got business in Dallas. I can't be caught up with no Fundies."

"Not a believer?" I ask, lifting my eyebrows. "Jesus saves, you know. Didn't you read that man's forehead?"

"I know who Prayer Donovan is," he snaps. "Only a fool don't recognize that monster." Another glance back at Donovan. "And sure as floods in Houston he's takin' us back to the reverend, am I right?"

All right, so maybe the first impression was a bit off the mark. Maybe he's not totally brainless after all.

"Can't promise anything until I know what you're holding," I say, turning my attention to the radio as if I'm already bored of him.

Seconds pass and Mr. Ponytail fidgets like a child holding his pee. I ignore him, feeling comfortably in control for the first time in days, watching him squirm out of the corner of my eye as I fiddle with the radio knob.

"Fine, fine," he snorts, his face twisted in frustration like a card player forced to bet his last chips on a crappy hand.

He cocks his head behind us. "That woman who was with me?"

"The fighter?"

He shakes his head. "No, not her. The other one. The young one."

"What about her?"

He tightens his lips and grimaces. It's the same expression you sometimes see on a market vendor's face, when he realizes he's been outfoxed in a deal and forced to give away something for nothing.

"She's Guzmán's witch," he finally spits out.

I stop turning the radio knob and look up at him. "What did you say?"

"She's Guzmán's truth-teller. The one who can see through lies. That's her back there."

"That's just a bullshit rumor," I mock. "Some made-up crap."

His eyes are fixed on me, unblinking and serious. "It's ain't no rumor. She's real. And I seen her do it, more than once."

Guzmán's reader? I'd heard the stories and blown them off as folklore, as foolish gossip. But there were other traders, traders who I know aren't fools, who swore she was real, swore she was Guzmán's ace in the hole.

I narrow my eyes at him. "So what's she doing out in the middle of nowhere?"

"She busted out of Guzmán's camp," he answers, "trying to make her way to Dallas."

"Why does she want to go there?"

"Beats me." He shrugs.

"So what are you, her guide?"

"That I am, but I sure as hell didn't sign up for it." He rubs his neck gingerly. "They put one of them collars on you, trader, and it ain't like you got a choice in the matter."

Now it's me who glances behind us. Donovan's finished with the tire change and making his way back to the Lincoln. Suddenly I wish I had more time to ask questions, to weed out bullshit from truth in the man's story.

"So why tell me?" I ask quickly. "Why not tell Donovan? You may have noticed I'm not exactly in charge around here."

"You can vouch for me with the reverend, tell him I ain't lying."

Vouch for him? Christ, he doesn't ask for much, does he? *Why don't you ask me to show you my tits while you're at it?*

This whole conversation is a waste of time. I turn my attention back to the radio, but not before I ask the obvious question, the one I don't expect him to answer. "And how do I know you're not lying right now?"

He looks at me as if I'm crazy. "Ain't you been listening to that radio, trader? The four of us is all they been talking about for the last half hour."

Donovan climbs into the driver's seat, puts the keys into the ignition. The motor rumbles to life.

"Heading out," he says into the hand radio.

We move forward in the falling light as I stare stupidly down at the radio sitting on my lap. Could I have really missed that much? It's possible. Exhausted and distracted, I'd stopped listening, really listening, some time ago. But now I study the chatter with careful attention, and within seconds I pick up words and phrases I failed to catch earlier.

And the more I listen, the more I understand, the tighter my stomach twists itself into a tight ball.

The ponytailed man isn't lying.

CHAPTER 13

The woman's name is Soledad Paz and she's Guzmán's truth-seer, his *reader*. She escaped Guzmán's camp right after he took Odessa, and now she and her three companions are on the run. No one knows where they are or where they're headed, and apparently the old desert snake has just about every truck, car, and motorbike in his army scouring the wastelands trying to find her.

It takes me all of twenty minutes to get this from the trade chatter, now that I'm actually paying attention. Secrets don't stay secret for long in Texas, thanks to my fellow gossipy traders, and you can't scramble a whole army without the who and what getting out pretty quickly. Trader ears are everywhere, always listening, which makes it something of a minor miracle that Guzmán has managed to keep this reader Paz under wraps for as long as he has. For the last couple years "don Flaco's reader" has been little more than folklore, a shadowy figure in Guzmán's inner circle. The secret weapon he uses to get the upper hand at every negotiation, to ferret out traitors in his midst, to see through the bullshit of every deal he makes.

I shift in my seat, imagining hundreds of vehicles out there somewhere, bearing down on us, getting closer by the minute. I glance over at the ponytailed man. He's listening to the chatter, too, though he's not trying to be obvious about it as he stares out the window. Hearing what I'm hearing.

He's a solo trader, this skinny, wrinkled man. Given his age, I never would have guessed it. Solo traders rarely make it past their twenties, given the occupational hazards of traveling the open wastelands alone. Mr. Ponytail must be as sharp and as wily as they come to have survived for so long.

Daylight fades. Behind us, most of the sun has disappeared already, only the smallest portion visible above the horizon. The land is flatter now and we no longer navigate around hills and valleys, instead maneuvering through forests of tall, thin pines. The air becomes thicker and heavy with humidity, a telltale of the coastal southeast. Donovan flips the headlights on, and the rest of the convoy follows suit. In the door's rearview, I watch as pairs of pale yellow lights flicker to life one after another.

"How much longer?" Donovan asks, startling me.

I click the radio off. "An hour, tops."

He doesn't ask about the radio chatter, thankfully. If he did, I'm not sure how I'd answer. When you're dealt new cards, the last thing you want to do is let anyone know how your lot changed. Best to sit tight, let the game unfold, and wait for the right moment to play your hand.

"Praise be to God," Donovan murmurs, but not in reaction to what I've said.

A few miles ahead of us, just visible above the treetops, a white spotlight sits atop a tall scaffold, shining in the darkness. A moment later I see three more towers, also with large, bright lights slowly scanning the surrounding forest. The beacons we've been waiting for.

*　　*　　*

As we approach the refugee camp at Lake Conroe, one

of the towers spots us and fixes its light on the Lincoln. For a few moments I'm blinded, and then through tearing, squinting eyes I see Donovan leaning out of the driver's window, waving up to whoever's in the tower. They must recognize him because the light quickly moves off of us, leaving spots and afterimages of tree trunks glowing in my vision.

Donovan takes his hand radio and dials it to another channel. He identifies himself, asks for directions and where to park. A voice comes back, loud and joyful, with some sort of glory to God welcome for him and the squad, then instructs him where to leave the vehicles. A couple minutes later the convoy parks atop a ridge overlooking the camp. I gasp as I take in the view.

"Good Lord," the ponytailed man marvels as the Lincoln rolls to a stop. "Look at 'em all."

Thousands of people. No, it must be tens of thousands. A teeming mass of humanity crowds the shores of Lake Conroe and overflows into the surrounding forest. I've never seen anything like it, never seen so many people in one place. An enormous clearing—no doubt recently razed to make room for incoming waves of refugees—on the opposite side of the lake is filled with a clutter of countless tents and small ramshackle shelters. Campfires are visible here and there, points of flickering orange light dotting the landscape.

Donovan climbs down out of the Lincoln, motions for the old trader to follow him. As he scoots toward the open door, Mr. Ponytail looks at me expectantly. *Do we have an understanding?*

I nod. "Keep your mouth shut," I mutter, "and I'll see what I can do." It's a bullshit line to keep him quiet. I still don't know what I'm going to do with the hand I've been dealt, and until I do, I don't want him giving anything away to try and save himself. Best he goes on thinking I'm his only way out of the mess he's in.

He nods back and then lowers himself out of the car. I

open the door on my side and step out, easing myself down to the ground. All around us there's an excited buzz in the air. People rush past like a flowing river, paying little attention to me and the newly arrived soldiers. Voices lift and strain in excitement.

"Baby, we have to hurry," a woman squeals. She carries a toddler in one arm, totes a rifle in the other. "We don't want to be stuck at the back where we can't see him." I catch the zealot's sparkle in her eyes, the same disturbing, intense giddiness I remember from the Fundie camp. The look is stamped over and over on other faces in the crowd, which bubbles with tears and grins and hoots and hollers. Emotions barely kept in check, a wild energy ready to be released.

Down below us, there's a raised platform on the lake shore that reminds me of a boxing ring without the ropes. A tightly packed crowd surrounds the front and sides, growing steadily larger at the edges as more arrive. Canoes and kayaks float near the back of the stage, hundreds of them, arranging themselves like puzzle pieces, covering the water so completely you could walk over from one edge of the lake to the other without getting your feet wet. In the center of the platform—which I now realize is a kind of stage—one of the tower spotlights focuses a brilliant circle of white light on a podium. No, not a podium, a pulpit. Anxious thousands wait for the speaker to arrive, for the Reverend Zachariah Wright. It has to be him, of course. There's too much crazy hanging in the air for it to be anyone else.

The passersby thin out a bit and I spot the four travelers, lined up and sitting on the ground in front of one of the Humvees. Their hands are bound behind their backs and a young girl stands in front of them with a bucket, giving them drinks of water with a ladle. Nipple Rings and Zara stand behind them, shotguns in hand. Zara stretches her neck to get a better view of the stage down below, her eyebrows lifted, her expression joyful and expectant.

I move my gaze to the young woman, this Soledad Paz, this runaway human lie detector who until today I'd blown off as silly folklore, right up there with jackalopes and chupacabras. I take a good look at her. Dull eyes peer out of a dirty face. Like the boy next to her and the ponytailed man, she seems exhausted. The tank woman scowls, her shoulders and arms bulging with muscles, furious eyes like those of a caged tiger. I look around, but I don't see Donovan anywhere.

"You stay put, trader," Nipple Rings calls over to me.

"What about my people?" I shout back.

"Brother Prayer'll come back for you," he answers, "and take you to the reverend."

Then the spotlight cuts out for a moment and the camp's suddenly pitch dark. Thousands of gasps escape from thousands of mouths. Then everything goes quiet. The air is charged with expectation.

As quickly as it disappeared, the spotlight returns, and down on the stage the Reverend Wright now stands behind the pulpit. A fat, linen-suited angel materializing from the darkness.

The crowd erupts into frenzied cheering, a sound so abrupt and loud it makes me wince. Arms wave around frantically, hats fly in the air in celebration. It's a raucous, deafening welcome for the Fundie preacher.

Wright stands patiently, the picture of serenity as he waits for the noise to die down. It takes several minutes before it finally does.

"Brothers and sisters in Christ," he announces, his voice reverberating through the night air, "I want to tell you the tale of the Republic."

I cross my arms. As if the torture of the past two days hasn't been enough, now I have to suffer a sermon.

Wright preaches his tale, a Fundie interpretation of the Republic's history. His voice rises and falls and pauses dramatically as he describes how the jihadees burned the foreign oil fields, touching off a global energy crash known simply as The Crisis. But the Lord's beloved Texas, he goes on, was blessed with abundant resources—huge stores of natural gas fields, the only viable fossil fuel left after all the oil fields were torched—and overnight our glorious land became wealthier than most nations. Wealthy enough to fund our blessed Secession.

My recollections from the history books I read as a kid are dim, but Wright's story seems to get the major points more or less accurate. As he goes on, the story gets sadder, recounting the doomed fate of the short-lived Republic of Texas thanks to a big drop in natgas prices, then the mass exodus north to the States. The crowd hangs on his every word like children rapt at a good bedtime story, quiet and still as he describes how the States eventually sealed off the border with walls, flying drones, and soldiers to keep out the flood of Texas illegals. And years later, in the ashes of our failed state, a new natgas technology—the solid, highly condensed pellets we've used for fuel and currency for generations—allowed a greedy few, the Bullock family and their cronies, to build a fortune and hoard it to themselves in their new, shining capital in Dallas.

Now he's really hitting his stride. His voice booms across the crowd, the lake, the entire camp.

"The Dallasites blaspheme and fornicate and worship their mountains of money as false idols while their soulless machines clean for them, cook for them, do everything for them. They live a life of wanton pleasure, but their time is coming to an end, their judgment is near." The preacher turns his eyes to the sky and spreads his arms wide.

"Brothers and sisters, the Lord has spoken to me. In a voice clear and beautiful and holy, He has revealed His sacred plan to His humble servant. He has blessed me with His vision."

The audience fidgets and murmurs, anxious for him to continue. He draws the moment out, gazing skyward, his arms outstretched, palms up.

"WE ARE THE CHOSEN ONES," he cries, "AND

WE SHALL DELIVER HIS VENGEANCE!"

The crowd explodes into a deafening roar, jolting me. I look over at Nipple Rings and Zara. They're both waving their arms to the sky, babbling in tongues. In front of them, the travelers sit frozen on the ground, awe and fear carved into their faces as they watch the mad cheering down below. Even the tank woman's stoic mask is broken, her brow furrowed, eyes worried.

*   *   *

Get your greenies and get the fuck out of here, Indigo Cruz. These are the words that repeat like a flashing neon sign inside my head as Donovan returns and leads me down the ridge to meet with Wright.

The reverend's speech ended a quarter hour ago, but the camp's still buzzing with a tangible, unsettling energy. I don't want to stick around a moment longer than I have to.

We find the reverend surrounded by dozens of fawning admirers, shoeless and ragged and dirty, pressing in around him. Voices screech with excitement, hands reach out for his magical touch, eyes run over with tears. Bodyguards prevent the adoring throng from smothering him entirely. They keep the crowd at a safe distance, but close enough so Wright can work them with meaningful stares, words of encouragement, and gentle touches from his sanctified hands.

"Lay your hands on me, Reverend!" someone next to me shouts as we get closer.

"God bless you for coming," another voice cries out. "God bless you!"

Wright lays his palm on a woman's forehead and mutters something into her ear, his eyes squeezed shut. She thrusts her hands and face to the sky, howling hallelujahs, her body shaking convulsively like she just stepped on an electric wire.

I watch the frenzied spectacle, amazed. He's been here what, a day? Two at the most? And already the entire camp seems to be under his spell, treating him like some long-awaited savior.

We stop short of the press of bodies, and Donovan waves to one of the bodyguards, who replies with a thumbs-up, then turns and says something to the reverend. The brim of Wright's hat tilts upward as he scans the crowd, a smile of recognition spreading across his face when he spots Donovan. I glance over at my companion. There's no answering smile on his stony face.

The bodyguards slowly maneuver the reverend through the crowd toward a small wooden shack with a flat-panel roof of corrugated aluminum.

"I have business I must attend to, brothers and sisters," he announces, placing his hand over his heart. "I thank you for your faith and fellowship."

After a lingering goodbye of handshakes and kisses to children's foreheads, Wright finally disappears into his hidey-hole. Donovan pulls on my arm and maneuvers me through the throng that's still milling about, and we make our way to the front of the shack, where a line of Fundie soldiers stand as a human barrier. One of them nods at Donovan respectfully and stands aside to let us pass.

Inside we find Wright alone and waiting for us. He strides over and grasps Donovan by the shoulders like a proud father.

"Brother Prayer," he beams. "Thanks to the Almighty. My heart's bursting with joy. I can't tell you how happy I am you're back."

The ice in Donovan's eyes seems to melt a bit. He nods but he doesn't return Wright's embrace, leaving his arms hanging at his sides.

Wright gazes at Donovan curiously, as if he's confused by his soldier's muted response. He releases Prayer awkwardly and then looks over at me. "Trader," he mutters, his voice suddenly low and cheerless.

I nod. *Lovely to see you, too.*

The reverend turns back to Donovan. "Is it true what they've told me, son? That you were successful in your mission?"

"Yes, Reverend."

The preacher removes his hat, sighs in relief. "I can't thank you enough, my boy. These people here can't thank you enough." Then Wright pauses a moment as if he's expecting a *you're welcome* or some other humble utterance from his soldier. Donovan stands there silent and unmoving, and again the curious look comes across the reverend's face.

He lays a hand on Donovan's shoulder. "They also told me your victory came at a terrible price," he says gravely. "I'm so sorry, Prayer. For all of them, for the boy."

At the mention of Remi, Donovan winces, almost imperceptibly.

"They're in a better place now, son," Wright consoles. "Their earthly worries are behind them. I know all you can feel right now is the loss, but they're with the Lord now. Let that knowledge give you some comfort in this time of pain."

Donovan exhales, his shoulders slumping in a surrender of sorts. "Yes, Reverend," he says.

For a long moment no one speaks, and I can feel Donovan softening under Wright's heavy presence, wilting like a water-starved plant under an overpowering sun. It's a remarkable power this man has, a remarkable thing to watch up close, Wright's ability to bend others to his will, the way he compels even the hardest of souls to yield to him. It's something far beyond a marketplace haggle or a con man's manipulation. Something powerful and inhuman. I can't wait to get away from it.

I clear my throat. "Reverend, my people?"

He looks at me, his smile fading a bit. "Fundies deal square, isn't that what you traders say?"

"It is," I answer, hoping today's not the exception.

"Your people are fine. They've been fed and treated well. Someone will take you to them shortly."

"Thank you, Reverend."

"No," he says, once again the magnanimous host, "it's you we have to thank, Trader Cruz." Wright moves over to me, reaches out a soft palm. "You have my sincerest gratitude. And if you ever need anything, I'm at your service." He squeezes my hand tight, a gloater's gleam in his eye.

I almost leave it all right there, leave without telling him what I know about the travelers, about the reader woman. After all, I'm in the clear, free to leave. I could just get my greenies and go home and have a much-needed drink or three and try to figure out what the next move is.

But I can't risk it. If I don't give her away, the ponytailed trader will, either voluntarily or with the assistance of a well-placed hammer. For all I know the old rat already has. Maybe he's somewhere right now, spilling his guts to whoever will listen. Stealing back the cards he gave me and playing them himself.

No, I can't stay quiet about her. Better to tell him now and stay on his good side, better not to leave the hand unplayed.

"There's one more thing, Reverend," I say.

Wright lifts his eyebrows. "What is it, trader?"

"It's about the travelers we picked up."

Sorry, Soledad Paz. It's your ass or mine.

CHAPTER 14

"How come you didn't say nothing about this before?"
Donovan snarls, glaring at me.

I take a step back, showing him my palms. "He only
told me just now, during the reverend's sermon." A small
lie, one I hope they don't catch. With the way Donovan's
looking at me right now, a little stretch of the truth feels
like a safer option than admitting I found out while we
were still on the road and held out on him.

The reverend removes his hat, runs a meaty hand over
his head as he weighs what I've just told him. "Did you
make some kind of arrangement with this man, Trader
Cruz? This guide of theirs?"

"I told him I'd put in a good word, but I couldn't
promise him anything."

Wright's eyes narrow skeptically. "You believe his
story?"

"It didn't strike me as made up. My take is he just
wants to be on his way and out of the whole mess." I leave
out the part about the chatter on the trade channels
confirming the ponytailed man's story. The last thing I
want to do is give Wright a reason to keep me here, grilling
me for hours over what I heard on the shortwave.

The reverend purses his lips, considering, then shakes his head. "A prisoner will say just about anything to gain his freedom, trader. I doubt this man's story has any truth in it, as much as I'd like it to be otherwise."

"Reverend?" Donovan says. I look over and he's pulling something out of his jacket. It's a small plastic bag full of small brown leaves. "I found this in the travelers' trunk."

He hands the bag to Wright, whose eyes widen as he turns it over, examining it. "Hierba," the preacher mumbles, then looks up at Donovan. "You think this is hierba?"

I'm lost at first, but then a ghost of memory comes to me, some piece of trader gossip about Guzmán's reader. Word was she had to use some plant before she could see lies. Some desert plant named hierba.

"One way to find out," Donovan suggests.

Wright grins, donning his hat. "I agree, son. And who knows, maybe some manna just fell right out of the sky into our hands." He then turns to me. "You stay here, trader. I'll have your people brought to you."

I look at him doubtfully, and he reacts with a generous smile, seeming to understand. "Y'all are free to go back home," he clarifies.

I sigh. "Thank you, Reverend."

Wright purses his lips. "Or you could stay here with us, enjoy some fellowship with your brothers and sisters in Christ."

I freeze for a moment, then he winks at me playfully. He chuckles and slaps my shoulder on his way out. "Vaya con Dios, trader."

After the reverend passes between us, Donovan looks at me, the knee-jerk anger from moments before now faded from his expression. He seems as if he's about to say something, his lips slightly parted, but then after an awkward wordless moment, he simply turns and follows the reverend out the door. A guard shuts the door and I'm alone. I close my eyes and stand there, feeling myself breathe deeply, trying to let the reality of my sudden freedom, my unlikely survival settle over me.

Not so fast, Indigo. You can relax once you're miles from here, not before.

The door flies open, startling me. Shooter stands in the doorway. "Well, looky here!" he exclaims. "I found me a trader."

Behind him are Hope, Pablo, and Jak. My greenies. Hope shoves past the boys and throws her arms around me, squeezing so hard she nearly chokes me.

She sobs into my ear, her breath warm on my skin. "You came back for us, Miss Indigo. Bless you for coming back."

I take her arms, unwrap them from around my neck. They all look unhurt, unmarked. Bright eyes and smiles on every face.

"You all okay?" I ask, averting my eyes from Shooter's bandaged hand. "How'd they treat you?"

Shooter nods at me. "Just fine," he answers, sliding the injured hand behind his back. "They fed us and let us be. Was kinda boring, honestly."

Something swells inside me, a strange, awkward churn of feelings. The turf boss in me wants to keep it all professional, to pat them on their backs and tell them they did good, keeping their heads on straight and sticking together. But there's another part of me that wants to open my arms and gather them all close to me like a mother hen with her chicks.

Hope wipes tears from her eyes. "I never been so happy to be wrong," she blubbers.

"Wrong?" I ask stiffly.

She sniffs, runs her sleeve across her nose. "Yeah."

"After you took off on the motorbike back at the camp," Jak says, "we thought...you know..."

His voice trails off, leaving the sentence unfinished but the thought clear: they didn't think I was coming back for them. I feel the fire of my surging emotions doused with a sobering bucket of water.

Can you blame them, Indigo? Shooter has every right to hate me. I stood by quietly while they hammered away at his hand, doing nothing to stop them. If he walked up right now and slapped me cold across the face, I wouldn't hold it against him. I wouldn't hold it against any of them.

"I know," I manage to say, trying to hide the shame in my voice, trying to keep my face from looking as if I've been kicked in the gut. "Come on. Let's go home."

*   *   *

"Do they know when that relief convoy's coming?" I ask Jak. He walks next to me with Pablo, Shooter, and Hope following close behind. A calm has descended over the shores of Lake Conroe, and the camp's much quieter now. Most of the refugees have retired to settle down for the night. The sharp chirping of crickets fills the breezy night air, a chorus punctuated by clanks and rattles of cookware as residents prepare meals of whatever they caught in the lake or shot in the forest earlier in the day. A few still wander about with tired, fallen expressions, dulled in the aftermath of Wright's fire and brimstone sermon. Bodies exhausted from shouting and stamping feet and waving arms.

"They say any day now," Jak answers.

"When did Wright bring you here?"

"This morning," he says. "You shoulda seen how they welcomed that preacher man, crowding around his vehicle and whatnot." He whistles. "You woulda thought he was Jesus himself come down from the clouds."

"You feel any of that divine inspiration?" I mock.

Jak bunches up his face as if he tasted something sour. "From that old crook? Please."

That's my boy.

"Miss Indigo, how are we gonna get back?" Hope asks.

Good question. I stop, put my hands on my hips, look around. "They got my truck around here somewhere." I grunt at myself. "Forgot to ask Donovan for my keys."

"*Prayer* Donovan?" Shooter says.

"Yes."

"I saw him just now when they was taking us to you," Pablo says. "He really the killing machine they say he is?"

"Killing machine nothing," Shooter argues. "They say he's a monster."

"The worst kind of monster," a gravelly voice behind us adds. The five of us whirl around to find Donovan glaring at us, his arms folded across his chest.

The greenies gasp and shuffle back and away from Donovan. He stares at me with that unreadable face of cracked, weathered stone.

"Come on," he says, dropping his arms to his sides, "they got your keys over yonder."

Donovan speaks into his hand radio and the greenies nervously trade glances as we follow, making our way to the far side of the camp. We pass row after row of ragged, threadbare tents and ramshackle lean-tos of weathered tarp, of pitiful scenes of refugees. Filthy barefoot children with sunken eyes, bony arms and legs. The old and sick, the dying and the nearly dead, splayed out on sagging cots.

Take a good look, greenies. This is what happens when you don't look out for yourself, when you trust that the place you've lived in all your life is a safe haven, when you don't have enough money squirreled away to build a wall between you and hunger, when you have faith that your family, that your town, that the Dallasites' protection, or anybody else's, can save you from the wolf at the doorstep. This is how you end up—starving and helpless and waiting for death—when you have faith in anyone or anything other than your own two hands, your own wits.

We come out of a tight cluster of tents and a large, deforested space opens up ahead of us. On the near side of the clearing stands Zara, her black braids dangling like a hangman's noose as she spins my keys around her finger, scowling as usual.

She nods at Donovan. "Brother Prayer." He doesn't return the greeting.

She glares at my heathen face and spits on the ground. Then she lets the keys drop from her hand as she turns and walks away.

I'll miss you, too, you crazy bitch.

I walk over and pick up the keys. As I stand, I turn them over in my hand, exhaling in relief as I feel the cool metal against my skin. In front of me, the clearing has a dozen or so torch poles scattered about, lighting up the area with a flickering orange glow. Hundreds of recently cut tree trunks dot the landscape like fresh scabs. Making room for more refugees, I think.

At the left edge of the clearing there are two long lines of people. Feet slowly shuffling forward, bony hands clutching metal bowls. Food lines. At the front of the lines, settled on smoldering beds of charcoal, sit large kettles, each manned by a Fundie ladling some kind of stew into the proffered bowls. Dozens of refugees sit scattered on the ground or atop tree stumps, busily feeding themselves with their fingers.

Zara walks among them, stalking the empty patches of ground between, her eyes bright with purpose, her voice booming. "And Jesus said unto them, I am the bread of life: he that cometh to me shall never hunger; and he that believeth on me shall never thirst!"

"Winning hearts and minds," I mutter.

The greenies walk up and stand behind me, quietly watching the feast of the starving.

"Blessed are those who hunger and thirst for righteousness, for they will be filled!"

Even more blessed are those who have a truck to get the fuck out of here. I turn to leave and Jak grabs my arm. "Look at that," he blurts.

"I've seen food lines before," I answer. "Let's go."

"No, not that. Over there, at the tree line."

I look over at the fringe of the clearing some forty yards away. Teams of workers bustle among the tall pines. Some work two-man saws back and forth, slicing steadily through the larger trunks. Others work alone, hacking away at the smaller trees with axes. Most of the activity, though, focuses on the felled timber. Hatchets chopping off branches, wrapping them into useful bundles for firewood and charcoal, arranging the bundles into piles.

Donovan pushes past me, peering over at the same spot. He walks forward a few steps, then stops suddenly. I look over again and realize most of the workers are children. Nearly all of them, in fact. The only ones who look older than ten are the ones chopping trees, doing the labor that requires the strength of adult muscles. A few Fundies with shotguns hover nearby, watching over them.

Then I see the manacles around the children's wrists and ankles, the long chains connecting them. A chill of horrible recognition jolts my body.

Slaves. *Child* slaves.

Donovan rushes across the clearing over to them and grabs a boy by the arm. The child cowers, throwing his arm out to protect his face as if he expects a beating, then he tries to pull away, crying and screeching. One of the overseers approaches and Donovan gives him an earful of harsh words I can't quite make out. The soldier looks nervously over at Zara.

"You do your duty, soldier!" Zara cries. "Don't let him interfere."

Donovan releases the child and stomps over to her. "What is this?" he roars. "What's going on here?"

Zara stands with her hands on her hips. "God's will," she answers, lifting her chin defiantly.

"God's will?" he spits back. "What are you talking about, woman?"

"Exodus chapter twenty," she says. "For I the Lord thy God am a jealous God, visiting the iniquity of the fathers upon the children unto—"

"You take them chains off right now, you hear me?" Donovan leans in close to her face, veins bulging from his neck, fists clenched. All around us, everyone's stopped what they're doing as they watch the spectacle. The food lines no longer inch forward. The sound of axes chopping falls silent. Even the ravenous diners stop eating, their hollow eyes staring up from their bowls.

Zara stands her ground, answers him by crossing her arms. Enraged, Donovan makes his way back over to one of the soldiers standing guard over the children.

"You do it," Donovan barks, pointing toward the children. "Unbind them young'uns!"

The shirtless Fundie again looks uncertainly over at Zara, who slowly shakes her head at him. The two other overseers approach, holding their guns at the ready, though their faces betray the same uncertainty as their partner's. Zara steps closer to them as she lifts a radio to her mouth and mutters into it. Her other hand is at her hip, the palm flattened against the butt of her holstered pistol, fingers outstretched and ready.

Donovan again orders the overseers to release the children. They don't move, seem to waver.

"You know your duty!" Zara bawls at them. The overseers slide the racks on their weapons, a cracking sound that echoes with deadly clarity in the night air.

The branded one whirls around, glares at Zara. She says nothing, hooking the hand radio back onto her belt. A dozen Fundie soldiers arrive at a jog, men and women, their heavily inked arms bearing rifles at the ready. When they see Donovan they hesitate, but Zara berates them into obedience and they quickly form a line, standing shoulder to shoulder, a barrier between the branded one and the enslaved children.

"What's happening?" Hope whispers to me.

My throat's too dry and tight to answer. I stare numbly at the chains around the children's feet and wrists.

Unwanted memories leak into my thoughts. My legs wobble and I feel as if the air's been sucked out of my lungs.

"Miss Indigo, what's wrong?" one of the greenies asks, I'm not sure which one.

Donovan rushes back over to Zara, an angry bull ready to trample her under his feet. She doesn't move as he approaches. She doesn't take a step back or even flinch as he presses his face in close to hers.

"You tell me right now what the hell you're doing!" he demands, poking her hard on the chest.

She looks down at his finger, then back up at him. "I ain't doing nothin' but the Lord's work," she says calmly. "Sins of the father and mother put them young'uns in bondage. I didn't. Ask the reverend."

"The *reverend?*" Donovan cries. "You better hope he don't find out them kids're in chains, woman." He pokes her again.

She slaps him across the face, hard. He stumbles back a step, as much from surprise as the force of the blow.

The amphitheater of the clearing is deathly quiet as everyone gawks at the unimaginable: Prayer Donovan struck like a child caught cursing in church. Zara glares at him in the same scornful way she did when the girl Miriam spoke out of turn. "It was the reverend hisself who locked them shackles on," she announces. "And he done it in the name of the Father, the Son, and the Holy Spirit."

"AMEN!" the line of soldiers shout, their cries an exclamation point to her statement.

Donovan stands, stunned, moving his gaze between the soldiers and Zara, his face twisted in confusion.

"The reverend?" he says, so quiet I barely hear him. He looks over at the children. "The reverend?" Then he shakes his head in denial, seems to regain his anger.

"I don't believe it," he growls. "He'd never do such a thing."

He removes the shotgun from his shoulder. Zara's eyes

widen and she steps back. *Cha-chuk!* Donovan racks the slide on his weapon, unaware of the soldier already closing on him from behind. "Sister Zara," Donovan barks, "you get over there and take off them—"

His head snaps forward as the butt of the soldier's gun crashes into the back of his skull. His legs go limp and he falls, landing facedown in the dirt, his weapon skittering across the ground. He lies on the ground at Zara's feet, unmoving, out cold.

Zara glowers over him for a moment, then spits on him. She looks over at me and the greenies, her face a mask of burning hatred as she strides over.

"Get on out of here, trader," she sneers, her face so close to mine I can feel her breath on my face. She clenches her jaw, shakes her head. "Why the good Lord saw fit to save your infidel hide while he took my little Miriam to her reward, it ain't my place to question. And it ain't my place to question the reverend's wisdom of letting you walk out of here, neither."

She takes a deep breath through her nose, her rage barely contained. "But even the faithful doubt, trader."

A Fundie soldier scrambles up behind her, gasping and out of breath. "Sister Zara," he pants, "it's fixing to start. They've got her to the neck."

She nods, but doesn't break her gaze from me. "Bring the young'uns. They gotta see and learn."

Zara pushes past me and the greenies and marches back toward camp. A few of the soldiers follow her, others gather up the manacled children. A woman soldier with braids like Zara's carries a long chain that she weaves through ankle shackles. I watch as more hands join her to help. Within a minute the soldiers are leading the children toward camp, their feet irons connected like fish on a trawl line.

"My God," Hope gasps, "look how many."

From the forest, more clusters of little heads appear, more ankles chained together. There have to be hundreds of them. Hundreds of child slaves.

They shuffle past us, the marching rhythm of their clanking chains a hollow heartbeat. Bony arms and legs, wrists and ankles chafed bloody, lifeless eyes cast downward. My legs feel frozen, my lungs leaden and airless as the children file slowly past. They disappear behind a jumble of tents and then they're gone.

Shooter tugs gently at my sleeve. "Come on, Miss Indigo, let's go."

His voice sounds impossibly far away. I'm still staring at the empty space where the children were a few moments ago.

He lightly taps my shoulder. "Miss Indigo?"

I gasp at his touch, snapping out of the dark cave of my stupor. The greenies are circled around me with wide eyes, waiting for me to say something. Hope brushes hair away from her eyes as she notices something behind me. "He's waking up."

I turn and look. A few yards away, Donovan's moving in the mud, coming around. He groans and pushes himself up off the ground, his limbs slow and clumsy. He manages to get himself into a sitting position, legs splayed out in front of him, and reaches behind his head. He winces, then takes his hand away. His fingers are wet with blood. He blinks slowly as he gazes around bleary-eyed, trying to get his bearings.

"We gotta go," Shooter insists.

"Just a second," I tell him, and I go over to Donovan, pulling a rag from my pocket. "Hold still," I say, kneeling down behind him and carefully dabbing blood away from the wound.

The branded one flinches when I press a bit too hard. "Sorry." I stand back up. "It's one hell of a lump you got back there, but the cut's small, not a gash." I hand him the rag. "Keep this pressed against it."

He looks up at me, nods tiredly, coughs. Then he tries to get up, but his legs fail him, and he stumbles sideways and sits back down hard. I reach down and grasp his upper arm, then lean backwards and heave against his bulk, helping him to his feet. He sways unsteadily, but manages to stay standing, gritting his teeth together as he presses the rag to the back of his head.

"How long was I out?" he slurs.

"Not long. Maybe a couple minutes."

He looks over to the tree line, squints in confusion. "Where are they?"

"She took them away."

He frowns. "Away where?"

I shrug. "Somebody else came up and said something was about to start, and…" I can't remember the rest.

"And 'they've got her to the neck,'" Shooter adds. "That's what they said."

Donovan's expression changes, his eyes widening in understanding.

Behind me there's a flare of orange light, and I turn to see a large torch pole firing up, back near the center of camp. The buzz and murmur of voices reach us. The sounds of an excited crowd.

"What is it?" Hope asks, her face suddenly illuminated, frightened eyes shining with reflected firelight.

I turn to Donovan. "What's going on?"

His mouth set in a grim line, he drops the rag to the ground and pushes past us, still on shaky legs. After a dozen steps he breaks into a wobbly jog, disappearing behind a jumble of tents.

We stand there for a moment, none of us speaking. "Miss Indigo," Jak finally says, his voice low and scared, "I think something bad's about to happen."

CHAPTER 15

My Ford's still parked up on the ridge where we arrived, on the opposite side of camp from where we're standing now. Whatever's about to go down under that big torch pole at the tent city's center, it's directly between us and our taxi out of here. We'll take the long way around, I decide, even if it means a few minutes longer of a walk. There's something unsettling about the crowd noise, something my gut tells me to steer clear of.

I lead the greenies through a maze of tents, using the towering torch pole as a reference point. We work our way through the narrow paths snaking through the jumble of makeshift dwellings, the dirt packed as hard as pavement by thousands of pairs of feet. The acrid smell of concentrated humanity—a sour, pungent brew of body stink, cooking smoke, and shit—assaults our noses. Many of the tents are empty, I notice, and the ones that aren't have mostly the old and the sick. A few try to get our attention as we pass.

"Are you my daughter?" an old woman croaks.

"Somebody's gotta take me to the pee ditch," a white-haired man sitting on the ground announces.

Others don't or can't speak, reaching out their hands to

us, pale and blue-veined and trembling. I don't look at them, keeping my eyes focused on the way forward.

The rumble of the crowd becomes louder, more frenzied, echoing the moments just before Wright took the stage for his sermon. Then a single voice rises above the excited din. I can't make out the words, but the resounding tone, the rhythmic ups and downs are unmistakably Wright's. The shepherd with his sheep. Or the wolf, depending on your point of view.

Minutes later the forest of tents and lean-tos thin out and we get a glimpse of what's going on. Hundreds of bodies crammed together surround the torch pole, its immense fire burning high above their heads, flames licking upwards into the night sky. The reverend's voice booms from somewhere deep inside the crowd. A few words crackle through and reach us.

"Refuses to repent…Mary-worshipper…May God have mercy on your soul."

Then a gap opens up in the sea of bodies and Wright's suddenly there, four bodyguards surrounding him like guardian angels. They move the reverend firmly forward through a gauntlet of outreached arms. As he emerges from the throng, he spots us and pauses. He smiles at me graciously, bowing his head and touching the tip of his hat with a genteel flourish. Then he's ushered away by his minders, vanishing into the chaotic mess of the tent city.

A few of the more enchanted followers trail after him, teary-eyed and overcome, but most wander back toward the torch pole, turning their attention back to the hanging or the tortured conversion or whatever other sick Fundie spectacle is taking place under the great ball of flame. The feeling in the air reminds me of my trip to Houston, of the moments before a public execution. The savage anticipation beneath ecstatic grins. The giddy blood lust.

"Come on, Miss Indigo," Hope pleads, pulling on my arm.

"Wait," I tell her, pulling my arm away as I spot a high-cut tree stump nearby. I clamber on top of it so I can see what's happening.

At the center of the churning mob, there's an empty space about ten yards wide formed by a ring of Fundie soldiers, arms locked to hold the crowd back. Inside the space stands the torch pole and what looks like a large rock on the ground.

Then I realize it's not a rock. It's someone's head.

They've got her up to her neck. The words come back to me as I recognize the tank woman, her entire body buried in the ground except for her head. She's moving, still alive, but she's been beaten and bruised badly, her face discolored and swollen.

Large mounds of rocks are scattered around the edge of the empty space. People jostle and shove to get within an arm's reach of the piles, grabbing handfuls of the fist-sized stones.

Stones. My stomach turns on itself as I realize what's happening. They're going to stone her.

The air teems with excitement, with madness. I spot Zara standing near the largest mound, holding a large rock in each hand.

"Go to the devil!" she shrieks, and then she rears back and heaves the first stone.

The crowd erupts into a screaming frenzy. Rocks fly through the air, hurtling toward the woman's head. Many miss the mark, but more than enough thud against their target with horrible force, ripping large cuts in her scalp, leaving hanging flaps of skin and hideous bleeding wounds.

I move my eyes away, unable to watch, and as I do I notice the reader Paz at the front of the crowd, surrounded by Fundie guards. She's on her knees crying hysterically, writhing and trying to break away from...

Donovan!

He has his arms around her, holding her in place. He leans down, his mouth next to her ear, telling her something. The girl finally stops resisting, her face frozen in agony, eyes fixed on the last violent moments of her companion's life. The longer I look, the less it seems like Donovan's restraining her and the more it appears he's trying to protect her, trying to comfort her as the sickening storm rages around her.

I step down from the stump, feeling the weight of the greenies' eyes on me.

"Come on," I tell them, avoiding their gazes.

"What was it?" Pablo asks.

"It's a killin', ain't it?" Shooter says flatly.

My silence is answer enough. "Let's go," I tell them.

We make a wide circle around the mob. The air has stilled, and the shouting and screaming has died down. The murder is done. It's quiet now, but the sounds of the woman's death still echo in my ears, the awful thuds of stones striking her head.

"There it is," Hope blurts out, pointing ahead of us.

My Ford rests at the top of the small rise. I've never been so relieved to see that run-down, dented piece of shit. My pace quickens, and I drive my tired legs faster as the path begins to slope upward.

We reach the truck and I slide into the driver's seat, feeling the familiar lumpiness under my rear. I grip the steering wheel, my fingers settling into the worn contours like a perfect-fitting glove. All four greenies try to squeeze into the front with me, even though they know there's not enough room.

"I'll get in back," Shooter says, then he exits the cab and climbs into the bed.

The engine snorts and chokes for an agonizing second, then rumbles to life. Sighing, I press the brake and put the Ford into gear as I scan the terrain at the bottom of the rise, looking for the quickest way out of camp. At the tent city's center, the stoning mob slowly begins to break up. Bodies drift back toward their tents, back to the business of waiting for the relief convoy. I maneuver the truck down the rise, carefully steering around freshly cut tree stumps.

We're halfway down when I spot Donovan sitting on a tree stump some fifty yards ahead of us. He's alone, his shoulders slumped. I brake, bringing the truck to a stop.

"Why are you stopping, Miss Indigo?" Pablo asks, his voice lifting with worry.

I gaze at Donovan sitting there, unable to take my eyes off of him. Shooter knocks on the window between the cab and bed, then slides it open and pokes his face through. "What's going on?"

Back over near the scene of the stoning, men with shovels dig the tank woman's body out of the ground. I look back down at Donovan, waiting for him to stand, to move, to do anything. But he just sits there, his posture that of a beaten prisoner.

"Be right back," I say, shifting the truck into park and opening the door.

"Where are you going?" Hope cries, reaching out and clutching onto my arm. Her nails dig into my skin like a frightened cat.

I turn and speak to all of them. "I'll be back, I promise. Just sit tight."

They start to protest, but I'm already out of the truck, making my way toward Donovan. He doesn't seem to notice me as I approach, his eyes fixed on the ground.

I stop a few feet in front of him. He sees my boots and his brow knits, a crease forming between JESUS and SAVES. He looks up at me, frowns.

"Thought you was gone already," he mumbles.

"Debt slaves," I tell him. "That's what they are, aren't they? Those children?"

He nods absently. "He just told me."

"Who told you?"

"The reverend. I was with him just now." He seems lost in his own head, as if only the smallest portion of his mind is aware of my presence.

"Since when do Fundies take debt slaves?" During my last trip to Houston, I hadn't seen anything like that, hadn't ever heard of the Fundies doing such things. With poppy farmers or fuck shack owners, sure, it was a known practice, a way of settling accounts. Children forced to work off some debt the parents owe, usually money borrowed to keep the rest of the family from starving.

"We don't," he says, then corrects himself, his voice dropping. "We didn't."

"Why is Wright getting into the money-lending business?" It strikes me as unnecessary, given Wright's monopoly on trade out of the Gulf and the vast amount of resources he controls. And why would he risk his holy reputation by becoming a slaver?

Donovan looks away from me, back down to the ground. "It ain't like that, trader."

"What do you mean?"

"He ain't *lending* nothing. It ain't no money debt them young'uns is paying off."

What other kind of debt was there? "Then what?"

"Sin."

Sin? For a moment, I don't say anything. "You're shitting me."

He looks up at me with cold, sober eyes. Definitely not shitting me.

"Sin meaning what? You take the Lord's name in vain and they lock up your kid?"

Donovan exhales tiredly. "He tried to tell me, tried to make sense out of it. Sins of the father and such. But there ain't no making sense of it."

Agreed. None of this makes any sense. "But why here? These people don't have a pellet to spare. They're starving."

The branded one shakes his head. "It ain't just here."

His expression carries too much weight, too much anguish, more than several dozen refugee kids can account for. I picture the children in chains, their bleeding wrists and ankles, the looks on their faces. Some wide-eyed with fear, still unable to understand what's happened to them, others with no expressions at all. The blank, soulless faces of those beaten into submission.

I grab a wooden crate lying nearby and set it in front of Donovan. "What do you mean not just here?" I sit down on the crate.

He sighs, dropping his eyes to the ground again. "You know about the problems in the Gulf?"

I shake my head. "Tell me."

And so he does, laying out the reverend's crisis slowly, his voice heavy with shame.

The reverend's power and influence, it turns out, is far less stable than it appears. While he has vast numbers of followers, Donovan tells me it wasn't his fiery sermons to the poor huddled masses that fueled his rise to prominence, it was his complex and far-reaching system of bribes and payoffs to Dallas loyalists. Wright lined the pockets of scores of police and Dallasite administrators, a payroll that over the years came to number into the thousands across southeast Texas. The reverend became the favored cash cow of the Dallas loyalists, who returned the favor of his largess by turning a blind eye to his sermons and his religious police, eventually allowing him—through their own greed—to rise to a position of incredible power. This much I knew already.

"Then one day the money stopped coming in," Donovan says flatly.

This, however, I wasn't aware of.

"We ain't sure how it happened," Donovan explains, "but the ships stopped coming to port, and the ones that went out never came back."

And *that* was the root of the Fundie leader's crisis. From his earliest days as a small-time preacher, the majority of Wright's income came from overseas trade with island nations in the Caribbean and a handful of countries in South America, energy-poor nations hungry for the seemingly endless supply of natgas pellets shipped out of the ports at Galveston, Corpus Christi, and a dozen other Gulf Coast trade hubs. Like everything else in the southeast, trade was nominally under Dallasite control, but Wright had side deals with boat skippers and he moved black market cargo on nearly every ship steaming in and out of Texas. It was a lucrative business for the reverend. While it lasted, that is.

Donovan describes how at some point roughly two years ago, all sea trade came to an abrupt stop. He remembers it as a sudden and devastating blow to Wright's operation, a huge, money-hungry monster that fed almost entirely on cash inflows from seafaring commerce. From one day to the next, it seems, the Fundie cause went broke.

"Some said it was a US blockade," Donovan recalls, "some said it was pirate vessels out of the Yucatan." He shrugs. "Nobody really knows."

Two years with *nothing* coming in. Christ, that's an awfully long time to tread water. An eternity for someone in Wright's position. Two years of scrambling for cash, of placating impatient officials who'd grown accustomed to their monthly payoffs. It's a miracle he survived six months, much less two years.

In hindsight, there were clues, of course. I recall the state of the Fundie camp before we left for Temple. Shoeless soldiers with ragged clothing, sunken eyes and bony limbs. There had been some gossip on the trade channels as well. The Fundies had become unusually tightfisted lately, hard to deal with, though no one suspected such a severe situation. It all makes sense now in light of Donovan's story. Wright's empire was bankrupt.

Donovan takes a deep breath. "We had some harsh words about it, about what to do." The debates became more heated, he describes, eventually turning into full-blown arguments. Wright wanted to mobilize his followers and take over Houston by force, wresting it from the hands of the Dallasites. It was working for Guzmán out west, after all, so why not for him? But Donovan disagreed. Houston wasn't some dusty little town out in Big Bend country, it was the Republic's most populous city outside of Dallas, equipped with a well-armed police force, not to mention gunbird support out of the capital, only one call away. The price in lives to win a bloody coup would be too high. Wright persisted, though, insisting there was no other way.

Donovan stops talking, his voice trailing off and leaving the story unfinished, but I can guess the rest.

"And that's why you retired?" I ask. "Why you left Houston?"

He kicks a rock with his shoe, watches it tumble across the dirt. "I thought he might not try to take the city without me."

And he was right. Without his top crusader at his side to lead the charge, the reverend balked and made no attempt to take Houston, and so far, still hasn't. But in the meantime, he found a way to make ends meet, a creative way to stave off his cash crisis and keep a precarious hold on his power base: child slaves whose parents pay off a "sin debt." Donovan tries, but he can't bring himself to describe it in detail, the very idea of it seems so painful to him. I get the drift, however, from the handful of words he manages to get out.

It's a scam only the most callous of minds could have come up with. First, the reverend's church officials call you out for your sin: gluttony, greed, envy, whatever. Next, they put a price tag on your misdeed, a financial punishment you the sinner have to pay to get square with the Jesus and His Fundies. Half a ton of natgas pellets, a silo's worth of grain, maybe your truck and tractor. And until restitution is paid in full, your child is kept in bondage, working like a Hebrew for Egyptians, chopping down trees, hunting game, fetching water.

Sin debtors. It's a hustle like nothing else I've ever come across, except one I dimly remember from an old book, something about medieval priests freeing souls from limbo for the right price. In the end, though, Wright's scheme, like the one from long ago, is nothing more than a shakedown, plain and simple. Blackmail with angel's wings.

And financially, it's a work of genius. Nearly a hundred percent upside income and very little expense. It's also more than just a cash windfall. The scam also supplies Wright with vast amounts of cheap labor, the only cost being a daily bowl of dog stew for each hungry mouth.

I think back to Wright dining on the huge meal the boy Remi cooked for him before we left for Temple. I see him sitting there in his air-conditioned tent, all smug and fat and in control. I feel my face warm with a rush of angry blood.

"But what about the relief convoy?" I ask, its looming arrival suddenly occurring to me. "Don't you think the UN might not appreciate the idea of children chained together by the ankle?"

Donovan shakes his head. "They don't never do nothing, trader. Don't never get involved."

He's right, of course. Up near the border, relief convoys bring food, water, supplies, and medicine, but they never dirty their hands in local politics or social affairs, no matter how brutal or bloody they may be. And their security forces have strict orders to protect relief staff only and no one else. The aid workers may be outraged by the sight of child slaves, and they may give the reverend a lecture and a good wag of a self-righteous finger, but aside from that they won't do a damn thing. They'll feed the hungry, tend to the sick, and then they'll leave.

"How long has this been going on?" I ask.

"Must have started right after I left, but I didn't know nothin' about it till this night, till we got here and saw them kids." His shoulders slump. "Seems they got young'uns in chains all over. Houston, Galveston, Beaumont, all up and down the coast."

He looks at me, eyes glistening. "He told me about it

without a lick of shame on his face, trader. Said it was the Lord's will."

I stand there, staring at the lifetime of sorrow and regret in his eyes. It must feel like a kind of death, suddenly realizing the man you've devoted your life to isn't the savior you always thought he was, when you see he's nothing more than a cheat in a preacher's costume. When you finally learn the only gods are false ones.

But there's no righteous indignation, no anger aimed at the child slaver. There's no more fuel in Donovan's tank, no more bullets in his gun. Where there used to be a warrior now sits the empty shell of a broken man. It's a heavy price he's paid. The price of faith in a faithless world.

I leave him there and make my way back to the greenies and the truck. I rub my wrists, remembering what I don't want to remember, when my own wrists were bound in metal cuffs, raw and bleeding.

Go home, Indigo. Just go home.

I reach the truck and pull open the door.

Hope sighs in relief, then nudges Jak. "Scoot over so she can get in."

I look at Shooter sitting on the edge of the bed. He tilts his head at me. "Something wrong, Miss Indigo?"

Yes. Now and always. With me and everything.

"You remember how to get back to our turf from here?" I ask him.

Shooter's face melts into confusion. "Sure, but why?"

"Listen," I say to him, to all of them. "I'll meet y'all back at home turf as soon as I can."

"What?" Pablo cries, his voice trembling. "You're not going back with us?"

I shake my head. "There's something I have to do."

"Then we'll wait here for you," Shooter insists.

"That's right," Hope agrees. The rest nod their heads, their expressions desperate with worry.

I fix them with a stern look, the kind that reminds

them who's in charge. "Listen, this isn't a suggestion or a request. You go on back there right now, or you can find yourself a new turf to work, you got me?"

That shuts them up. Shooter climbs down off the bed and gets behind the wheel.

"Shooter, you can't drive with your hand—"

"I'll be fine, Miss Indigo."

I lift my chin at Jak. "You drive."

Jak shrugs. "Shooter's the best driver between us, Miss Indigo," he says sheepishly. "One hand or two."

The other two nod their heads in agreement.

"Fine." I close the truck's door.

"Don't forget," I tell Shooter, "due east until you hit 45, then—"

"Then it's a straight shot north," he interrupts. He grips the wheel with one hand, the other resting on his lap, still wrapped in a bloodstained bandage. He notices me looking at it, then moves it to his side where I can't see it.

Shooter nods at me, squeezes my shoulder with his good hand. "I'll get us there. You be careful, Miss Indigo."

He puts the truck into gear and pulls away. I watch the Ford crawl to the bottom of the rise, then it turns eastward and disappears into the pines.

*　　*　　*

"I never told you my story, you know."

Donovan looks up at me, knits his brow in confusion. I sit down again on the crate.

"What did you say?" he grumbles.

"You told me what happened to your town, how the reverend saved you."

"Why are you still here, trader?"

I don't answer. Over at the big torch pole everyone's gone. Hundreds of stones lie about, and there's a large hole where they dug out the body. The great flame has begun to die out, the fireball already burning with half the size and intensity as minutes earlier.

"We were farmers up north," I begin, "around Denton. Mostly wheat, some corn. Had some cattle, too. I guess around a hundred head or so."

Donovan stares at the ground.

I keep going. "Farming's not like trading. On a farm you're stuck to that piece of land and whatever it produces, good times and bad, wet years and dry. A trader doesn't have to worry about all that. If you're smart enough to know what folks are going to need, you can make a pretty good living trading. Buy low, sell high. Supply and demand. And if things get lean, you just pack up and find someplace better."

"You got a point, trader?"

Do I? I'm not sure, but I continue anyway. "A farmer hopes and prays for the right amount of sunshine and rain. No trader in their right mind would sign up for such a chancy deal, putting their faith into something other than their own smarts."

I swallow at the memory of my last summer on the farm. "When I was nine, a tornado hit our land about a month before harvest. Knocked down our house, left the wheat fields looking like they'd been carved up with some giant knife."

I can hear my mother sobbing, see her falling to her knees when we crawled out of the cellar and got our first look at the hectares of stripped-bare ground where our crops had stood an hour before. My father standing next to her, hands on his head, his mouth hanging open as he stared out at the razed fields.

"That's all it takes, you know," I tell Donovan. "When you're a farmer, one piece of bad luck, one fuck you from the gods, and one day to the next you're scrounging out a living. Next thing you know, you find yourself asking your kin and your friends for loans to get by, and they give them to you, but you can never quite get the land to produce the same again. So then you take on more debt to pay off your old ones, but this time you take out loans from strangers, and the strangers don't let you miss a payment like your family and friends did. You work yourself to death to pay off that debt, but the land doesn't help you, the weather doesn't help you. No matter how hard you pray, no matter how much faith you have that things are going to turn around someday, you can't get that boot off your neck."

I feel Donovan's eyes on me now, feel him listening.

"After a year of scrambling and watching your family slowly starve, a man appears at your farm one day. He has a solution to your woes, a way to pay off all that debt with a simple trade." I turn and look at Donovan. "You've got four children, the man said to my father. I'm only asking for one of them."

For a long moment neither of speaks. "You were a debt slave?" the branded one finally asks.

I nod.

"How long?"

"Eight years."

"Doing what?"

"You don't want to know," I say. And I don't want to remember.

"And then they finally paid off the debt, your family?"

I shake my head. "I'd still be in chains if I'd have left it up to those fools, all their stupid praying for rain and hoping for some miracle." I feel the anger rising up inside, the fury that's always there, simmering in the pit of my stomach. "I paid it off on my own. Taught myself to trade, to make my own money on the side. Steal food in the market, sell it in the alley at half price. Rent out my bed while I slept on the street. Stealing, hustling, doing whatever I had to."

Again, a long, wordless moment passes. I squeeze my eyes shut, pushing the memories out of my head. All those months and years squirreling away money, learning all I could from books I found in old ruined houses or stole from the bazaars. Making sure I had book smarts to go with street smarts so I'd never get trapped by ignorance like my parents had, so I'd never have to depend on anyone, never have to rely on something as stupid as faith or hope or some invisible man who wasn't there, and if he was he didn't give two shits about anyone's suffering.

"Why are you telling me all this?" Donovan finally asks.

I lean in closer. "We can't let Wright have that reader woman," I say. "We've got to get her out of here."

He sighs. "What are you talking about, trader? He's already got her."

I fix my eyes on his. "She's been Guzmán's secret weapon all this time. She's the reason he's been able to grab so much land out west. Think about it. He never loses a battle, and every trader knows the man never gets the short end of a deal. Three years ago, he was a just another West Texas sand bandit. Now he holds thousands of square miles and who knows how many natgas fields. Nobody's that good, Donovan, and nobody's that lucky. It's all her, it *has* to be. She's the power behind the power. That's why he's got a whole army out looking for her."

He purses his lips, considers. "Maybe you're right, but what does it matter?"

I lean in closer. "War is coming. You know it, I know it. And when all hell breaks loose, do you really want her in Wright's hands? You really want *him* using that gift of hers to tip the odds in his favor?"

He looks away from me. "Too late to do a thing about it."

I reach out and grab his forearm, squeezing it urgently. "Prayer," I plead, "you know what he is now. We both do. And we just handed that reader woman over to him—to a child slaver—on a silver goddamn platter. If he uses her to take the Republic, it's going to be on us."

He pulls his arm free of my grasp. "You think she'd be better off with Guzmán or them Dallasites?"

"I think she'd be better off anywhere but where she is

now."

"You're asking me to betray the reverend." *The man who saved my life.* He doesn't say it, but the words are there, behind his eyes.

I shake my head. "That's not how I see it."

"No? How do you see it, trader?"

"The minute he turned the locks on those chains, he turned his back on you, on everything you believe in."

Donovan sits there for a while, staring out into the darkness. He doesn't say anything for a long time. Then he takes a deep breath in through his nose and exhales from his mouth in a long, slow blow.

"What can we do?"

I reach into my pocket, pull out the hand microphone and show it to him. "I need the radio."

CHAPTER 16

What are you doing, Indigo Cruz? I don't have a plan to get this truth-seer woman out, I'm surrounded by people who'd love nothing more than to see my head on a spike, and I need a bath like nobody's business.

Donovan and I trudge back up the rise toward the squad's vehicles. My mind races, trying to come up with something, some way we could steal this Paz woman out of here. It feels like the longest of long shots, one step below a fool's errand.

First things first, Indigo. You have to get the lay of the land, have to find out what's going on out there beyond the camp, find out if anyone's spotted Guzmán's rolling cavalry.

"Guzmán's out looking for her?" Donovan blurts out from behind me after I give him the news. "You didn't say a thing about that to the reverend."

"Can of worms I didn't want to open. You think he would have let me go if I'd said something?"

"Maybe not," Donovan admits.

"Maybe nothing. He would have chained me to a radio with a gun to my head until I found out everything I could."

"Could have told *me*, at least," he snorts.

"Yeah, well, you weren't in my good graces at the time."

"Lord above, trader, they might be bearing down on this camp *right now*," he scolds.

"Keep your voice down, will you? They never saw the reader woman's car, and they were never trailing us. There's a lot of land out there to cover before they'd come looking this far east. I just want to make sure."

We reach the top of the ridge. Except for my truck and one of the Humvees, all the squad's vehicles are there, including, to my relief, the Lincoln that hopefully still has the radio sitting on the front seat. Three men with shaved heads and long braided beards stand guarding the vehicles, semiauto rifles in their hands.

"Let me do the talking," Donovan mutters.

Be my guest.

"Evening," Donovan greets them. When they recognize him, their hard stares melt into awe.

"Brother Prayer," gasps one of them, a man with intricate, spiraled face tattoos. He throws his weapon over his shoulder and strides over. "We praised the Lord when we got word you made it back safe." He shakes Donovan's hand vigorously, his eyes sparkling with admiration. I blow out a breath, relieved to see Zara hasn't already turned the entire camp against him.

"Thank you, brother," Donovan answers. Then the man turns to me and his smile fades into that special look the Fundie faithful reserve for the especially soulless like me, an expression that manages to be both self-righteous and batshit crazy at the same time. By now I've gotten used to it. In fact, if they welcomed me with anything else, I'd probably be suspicious.

Spiral Tattoos speaks to Donovan, but he doesn't move his eyes off of me. "Is there something I can help you with, brother?"

"Left my shortwave in the Lincoln," the branded one answers. He moves to step past, but the guard quickly shuffles backwards, moving his body between Donovan and the car, blocking him. Donovan jolts to a stop, puzzled.

"I'm sorry, brother," the guard says. "We ain't supposed to let nobody near the vehicles. Reverend's orders."

"I ain't gonna steal the car, son," Donovan assures him. "Just need to reach in the window and take out my gear."

The guard's expression is nervous, unsure. He glances over at his two partners. They exchange awkward glances, as if each of them expects the other to say something.

"I'll fetch it for you, Brother Prayer," the shorter guard suggests, and he trots over to the Lincoln.

"Much obliged," Donovan tells him. "It's on the front seat."

"Yes, sir," he answers as he climbs onto the running board and pulls open the door.

The tall guard's hand radio crackles. He unhooks it from his belt and lifts it to his face. "Post three, I read you, over."

The shorter guard hops down off the Lincoln with the shortwave under his arm.

A voice comes from the hand radio, the words distorted and unclear, but the voice unmistakably Zara's.

"Brother Prayer's with us," the tall guard replies. "Got that woman trader with him, over."

Zara barks back immediately, but I can't make out everything she's saying. "What…she…still here…?"

"Affirmative," the taller guard says, watching me as he speaks. "She's still here, over."

I feel a dampness under my arms, a tightness in my throat.

"What…doing?"

The shorter guard approaches, hands the shortwave to Donovan.

"Getting his radio from the Lincoln, over," the tall

guard answers. Then he winces and pulls the radio away from his ear as an explosion of static and word fragments erupts from its tiny speaker.

I give Donovan a worried look. He nods at me, the smallest downward motion of his chin. *Oh, Christ.* My heart thuds against my chest as he thanks the shorter guard and tucks the radio under his arm.

The tall guard dials down the volume on the radio. "Lord," he mutters, "that woman's voice could wake the dead." Then he speaks into the radio again. "Come again. I didn't get your last, over."

Zara's reply is too low to make out, but whatever she says makes the guard's eyes widen. He whips his gaze over at us, the radio falling from his hand and thudding against the ground.

"Get that shortwave back!" he shouts.

Then several things happen almost at once, actions mashed together in the space of a second or two. Donovan smashes a fist into the face of the shorter guard, then pivots and throws his leg up, his shin bone crashing into Spiral Tattoos' jaw, sending the man's head snapping backwards, eyes rolling white into his head. Both men fall, their bodies limp like their bones have suddenly lost all form. Donovan shoves the radio into my gut and barks at me to run.

I look down stupidly at the radio in my hands.

"Run, trader!" Donovan yells. I scramble away, running for the cover of a nearby clump of pine trees.

As I reach the trees, I glance behind me. Donovan and the tall guard are locked together, fighting and rolling across the ground.

I run wildly through the woods, in no particular direction other than away from camp. Within seconds I'm blind, the darkness of the dense forest swallowing the glow of the camp's torch fires. Pine needles scratch my face, and I stumble and over logs and shrubs. My lungs begin to burn with the effort, forcing me to slow to a jog. My eyes adjust to the dim moonlight, and the forest takes shape around me, hazy outlines of pale white light. I check over my shoulder a few times, but I don't see anyone following. After another couple minutes, my legs aching and complaining, I pause to catch my breath. Dizzy and spent, I bend over at the waist and take huge, gulping breaths until the lightness in my head goes away.

I stay there for a moment, not moving and listening to the forest. Insect sounds, frogs croaking near the lake, but nothing else. No rustling of leaves. No running footsteps, no shouting.

I sit down against a tree trunk, the rough bark hard against my back. With the radio on my lap, I plug the microphone into the jack. Volume down to zero, I flip the power switch, then bring the radio up onto my shoulder, the speaker inches from my ear. Slowly, I dial up the volume until I hear the faintest buzzing of static, then I start moving through the channels, scanning the airwaves for traderspeak. It takes me a few minute of searching, but I finally find an active channel. I wipe the sweat from palm onto my pants and grab the microphone. A quick call for help and then I'll start moving again.

"Drop it," a voice growls from the darkness, startling me. The tall Fundie guard steps out from behind a thicket.

Shit.

He creeps forward, moonlight glinting off the barrel of his shotgun. "Get your hands off that radio," he sneers, stepping forward. I set the radio on the ground next to me.

"Stand up," he orders, breathing heavily. His face is bruised and bloodied. I wonder what happened with Donovan.

"I said stand up, woman," he repeats.

I get to my feet, raising my hands like a thief captured in the act. "All right, take it easy."

He glares at me, and I can feel the anger coming off him like heat from a torch. "I never thought I'd see the day," he seethes, "when a heathen trader corrupts Prayer

Donovan."

I drop my hands, too tired to keep them in the air. Is he still alive back there? I picture him back on that ridge, lying in the dirt, not moving.

Behind the Fundie, there's an explosion of leaves and branches as something bursts out of the underbrush. *Clunk!* The Fundie's face twists with pain for an instant, then he drops the shotgun and collapses to the ground.

"Sleep tight, motherfucker." Shooter! The greenie stands over the unconscious guard, glaring down at him. In his good hand, he holds the old baseball bat I keep under the driver's seat of my truck.

"Shooter," I gasp. "What…how…?"

He looks at me, smiles. "Jesus, that really felt good."

The rest of the greenies emerge from the forest, their eyes fixed on the fallen Fundie.

"Is he dead?" Pablo asks.

"Nah, just KO'd," Shooter answers, nudging the sleeping Fundie with his boot. "Tie him up."

Stunned, I watch as they bind the Fundie's hands and feet together and gag him. Hope picks up the soldier's shotgun.

"What are y'all doing here?" I demand. "You ought to be miles away from here by now."

"You're welcome," Shooter mocks.

"I told y'all to get back to home turf," I snap.

"You did, Miss Indigo," Shooter says. "But we gave it a second thought, figured you just might need a hand." He lifts his eyebrows at me. "You reckon we made the right call?"

Well, shit. Not a lot you can say to that, is there, Indigo?

Hope whirls around, pointing the shotgun at something in the darkness. A tall figure emerges out of shadows. It's Donovan.

"Hope," I say, "it's fine. Put it down." The greenie hesitates for a moment, then lowers the weapon.

As Donovan approaches I get a better look at him, and

he's not looking good. The moonlight reveals a face that's beaten up worse than the guard's. One of his eyes is nearly swollen shut and his nose is badly broken, bent grotesquely out of shape.

Donovan notices me staring and gingerly touches his brow. "Is it that bad?"

"Not at all," I lie. He looks like he just ran his head through a meat grinder.

He points down at the shortwave on the ground. "You get anything on that yet?"

"Didn't get a chance," I answer, kneeling down and reaching for the radio. I place it on my thigh, increase the volume a bit. After a few moments I catch a few words, then phrases and whole sentences. There are two of them talking, and they're both in a panic. Chattering back and forth about the best way to go east, whether or not they should risk crossing the drones routes up near Dallas, how much time they have left to get out.

"What are they saying?" Jak asks.

"Shhhh!" I wave him quiet.

I take the microphone, clear my throat. "Seven eight two, what do you do?"

The channel goes quiet for a couple moments, then one of them responds, asking for my location. I tell him I'm at Lake Conroe.

A jolt of fear shoots through me when I hear the answer back. I drop the microphone.

"What is it?" Donovan asks. "Tell me."

I turn to him, then look at the greenies. "Where'd you park the truck?"

*　　*　　*

"What do you mean we can't go back to home turf?" Jak cries.

"Yeah, I thought you *wanted* us there," Hope adds.

Shooter climbs into the truck and I shut the door

behind him.

"Why won't you come with us?" Pablo begs, his voice shaking.

They're all talking at the same time, peppering me with questions there's no time to answer.

"Listen to me, all of you," I shout, shutting them up. "They spotted Guzmán's trucks in College Station not two hours ago, heading east in a hurry. My turf's not safe right now, and neither is the ground I'm standing on."

I pass the shortwave and the microphone over to Hope. "You get hold of somebody at our turf, tell them what's happening, tell them to get out of there until all this blows over." She looks down anxiously at the radio, then at me. "You can do it," I assure her. "Tell them get to the east as quick as they can. Got it?"

She bites her lip, nods. "Got it, Miss Indigo."

Jak says: "But what are you going to—"

"You just get yourselves of here, you hear me?" I interrupt. "I'll catch up as soon as I can."

They fall silent, fear and confusion on all their faces. All except Shooter.

"We'll be all right," he says, his voice cool, controlled. He gazes at me with clear eyes, full of purpose. A greenie no longer, it seems.

I squeeze his shoulder, and he reaches up and presses his hand—the good one—on top of mine.

"Go," I say, and he nods, turning the ignition.

I back away from the vehicle. Donovan stands next to me as we watch them drive away. I hold up my hand just before they disappear into the forest, all but certain I'll never see them again.

*   *   *

We are fucked. So fucked. Off the charts, immeasurably fucked.
Donovan and I hurry back toward camp through a crowded maze of pine trees, both of us clueless as to what

we'll do when we get there, as to how we'll wrench this truth-seer woman out of Wright's grip.

And what if we *do* manage to get her out? What then? How far can she run before Guzmán's army catches up with her?

High above our heads, the four tower spotlights rotate, throwing circles of light on the surrounding forest in slow, lazy arcs. We reach the ridge with the vehicles. The two guards Donovan took out earlier are gone.

"Where are they?"

Donovan shakes his head. "I don't know."

So very fucked.

Forget it, Indigo. There's no time to worry about them now, no time to worry about anything.

"Where are they keeping her?" I ask.

"Over there." He points to a group of large tents, just beyond the clearing where they stoned the tank woman.

"We gotta keep out of sight," Donovan says.

Most residents seem to have retired for the night; only a few campfires scattered here and there are still burning.

"Think they're looking for us?"

"Could be," Donovan answers. "Wouldn't bet against it."

"That's reassuring."

"Here, take this." Donovan hands me a Glock he took off one of the guards. "Full clip, but I ain't got no extras, so if there's a firefight, don't go and get trigger-crazy, you understand?"

I nod. *So fucked.*

Donovan nudges me with his elbow, then nods down toward the bottom of the ridge, where two men with rifles over their shoulders stand facing each other. One of them speaks into a hand radio. I freeze, suddenly aware that we're out in the open, and all they have to do is look up the ridge to spot us.

"Get over here," Donovan hisses behind me. I turn and see him already hiding, crouched down behind one of the Humvees.

"THERE, UP THERE!" I whirl back around. One of the men is pointing up at me. The other one's shouting into the radio. "Northeast ridge, northeast ridge, we got eyes on the woman!"

In the next moment a white light envelops me with sudden, violent brilliance. I squeeze my eyes shut, throw my arm over my face.

Run, fool, they've got the spotlight on you.

I feel Donovan's hand clamp around my arm. He yanks me out of the light. Blinded, I flail around, blinking tears away.

"Get down," Donovan snaps. My vision's filled with flashing spots. In front of us, the circle of light zigzags around the ground, trying to find me again. We duck down behind the truck.

The two men appear, moonlit silhouettes with rifles, standing in front of the same truck we're hiding behind, no more than twenty feet away.

"See where they went?" one of them pants, winded from the run up the ridge.

"They can't have gone far," the other one answers. He raises the radio to his mouth. "Tower three, bring your light around to these trucks so we can see—"

I flinch at a sudden whizzing in the air, followed by a loud, meaty thud. The man with the radio drops to the ground. His partner looks down at him, opens his mouth to speak, but before he can say anything there's another thud and the second man spins awkwardly and falls to the dirt. They both lie there motionless.

"Sniper," Donovan whispers. "Get your head down."

"Sniper?" I gasp.

There's a rattle of automatic gunfire from somewhere deep in the forest, and then I hear screaming and panicked voices from the light tower. I look up just as the spotlight's shot up, sending shards of glass flying, the light doused instantly. Dark figures scramble about the scaffolding at the top of the structure. Shouts and confusion. Then something catches my attention from the corner of my vision, a bright flare of orange coming out of the treetops like a huge firefly, zooming in a straight line for the tower.

An orange ball of fire suddenly engulfs the top half of the tower, quickly followed by a booming shock wave that rattles my insides. I instinctively drop down behind the truck, my belly to the ground. A moment later Donovan pulls me up to my knees. He's saying something to me, but I can't hear him over the ringing in my ears.

"You all right?" he repeats.

"Yeah."

I look back to the tower, or rather to the spot where there used to be a tower. In its place is a mangled mess of scaffolding, maybe ten feet high, its uppermost tips smoldering. The rest of the structure lies scattered around as small, burning pieces of metal and smoking debris.

For a long moment everything's quiet. No gunfire, no shouting, nothing. Then from somewhere deep inside the camp comes the whine of a hand-crank siren. An alarm being sounded.

"What was it?" Donovan asks, rising up to get a better look at the burning mess. "Did you see it?"

"RPG," I answer, brushing dirt off the front of my shirt.

He whips his gaze to me. "You sure?"

I nod. "I saw it come out of the trees." We stare at each other, both knowing what it means.

Guzmán's army has arrived.

CHAPTER 17

The quiet moment doesn't last longer than a few seconds. There's another boom and we both flinch as a second explosion lights up the sky above the camp. Another tower's been struck.

From the forest behind us there's more gunfire. Bullets strike against the vehicles. I recoil with each metallic thud.

"Let's go," Donovan barks, pulling at my arm.

We scramble down the ridge, away from the gunfire. The embankment's slope has become a hell of smoldering pieces of metal and charred human limbs. As we reach the bottom, the camp is already swarming with panic. Families rush about, fear and confusion on their faces. Parents clutch small children, running for the safety of the center of camp. Others huddle together, frozen in terror. Fundie soldiers are assembling in small groups, their faces as bewildered as those of the refugees. Squad leaders shout into hand radios.

Donovan and I knife our way through the chaos. Two explosions flare in quick succession, both on the camp's opposite side. Deep booms that rattle my bones. A burst of terrified cries. The last two light towers are gone.

Then suddenly it's dark, and there's only the dim,

patchy glow of barrel fires left to light our way. I follow Donovan automatically, unsure of where we're going or what we're doing.

"We can still get her out," he tells me, lifting his voice above the rising din of frenzied shouts.

The reader! My brain's so scrambled with animal panic, I'd momentarily forgotten about her. *Keep your head on, Indigo.*

The part of my mind that's not whirling realizes that, yes, we can still get her out. In fact, with all the screaming, scrambling confusion, this very moment may actually provide us with our best shot. If we live longer than the next few minutes, that is.

We hurry, bumping and shouldering our way through a flowing river of bodies. Children wail, terrified. Adults yell, their voices straining and crazed. In the distance the *pop-pop-pop* of automatic gunfire comes in short bursts.

We cut through a row of shanties and then Donovan suddenly stops, holding out his arm so I don't run past. I pant, out of breath, too winded to speak.

"That's it," he tells me, nodding at a large tent about twenty yards ahead. A single guard stands in front of the door flap, gripping his shotgun tightly, shifting his weight from one foot to the other. He looks nervous, jumpy, like he'd welcome any excuse to abandon his post.

"Stay here," Donovan yells, and in the next moment he disappears into the cluster of bodies between us and the guard.

The crowd surges and suddenly there's so many panicking refugees running back and forth I can't see what's happening. I spot a folding chair a few feet away, next to an abandoned campfire, and step up onto it. I pick out the guard again, and now Donovan's standing in front of him. It looks like they're arguing. The guard shakes his head vigorously, then Donovan's elbow strikes him on the temple, catching the guard completely unaware. It's a quick, powerful blow that sends the guard staggering forward and flopping face-first to the ground. In the riot scene surrounding us, no one seems to take notice. Donovan reaches for the shotgun and disappears inside the tent.

A moment later he emerges with Guzmán's reader, this Soledad Paz, and the boy she was traveling with. He speaks to them, pointing urgently in the direction we just came from. I hop down off the chair, but before I can make my way over, Donovan's already pushed his way to me through the crowd.

But Paz and the boy aren't with him. "Where is she?"

"I gave her keys to one of the Humvees," he answers. "Come on, let's go. We'll get out of here with her."

The bursts of gunfire are louder now, and more frequent. People rush past us, a mayhem of panicked faces.

Then a woman in front of us stumbles to the ground. At first I think she tripped, but then when she doesn't get up I notice the gaping exit wound on the side of her head, a pool of blood expanding outward, soaking into the dirt. Shrieks fill the air and the crowd scatters in every direction, revealing more victims lying on the ground.

"Trader!" Donovan shouts, pulling me toward a pile of sandbags a few yards away. We dive behind them, away from the incoming fire. Green tracers are suddenly everywhere, zipping through the darkened camp. Two rounds hit the sandbags with heavy thuds.

We're cut off. We can't follow after the Paz woman without walking straight into the line of fire.

"We're gonna have to go around," Donovan says, racking the slide on the shotgun. A squad of Fundie soldiers sprints past us, firing and screaming war cries.

"Now!" Donovan barks, and then we're moving. We crouch low and run in the opposite direction of the attack. I follow close behind, keeping my eyes locked on his back. The gunfire seems to be coming from everywhere now, from all sides.

We run, dodging tent poles and ducking under support

ropes. With so little light, I stumble over unseen obstacles, striking my shins against pieces of cookware and tripping over heaps of trash. We come upon a small clearing at the edge of camp and stop. It's a quiet, secluded corner of the tent city that doesn't appear to be under siege. For the moment, at least, we seem to have escaped the worst of the firefight.

Donovan turns to me, breathing heavily. "All right," he pants, "we gotta cut straight back this way and—"

Something catches his eye, and he shifts his gaze beyond me to the clearing. I turn and look. In the middle of the open space, barely visible, a group of children huddles together, squatting on the ground. One of them sees us and stands up, a silhouetted shape of a child no more than ten years old. The shadow raises a hand in our direction, a chain hanging from the wrist.

A chill of recognition shoots through me. The debt slaves. They've been left on their own, abandoned by whoever was watching over them.

Donovan sprints past me, toward them.

"Prayer!" I shout, but he doesn't stop, doesn't break stride. In the next moment he's there with them, kneeling, his arms furiously working at something on the ground.

Three of the children suddenly come running toward me, still connected by their ankle chains. They duck down behind a nearby pile of sandbags. Then another three, also chained together, join them.

"It's okay, it's okay," one of the older ones, a girl, murmurs. She clutches a young boy, hardly more than a toddler, tight to her chest, trying to comfort the sobbing child.

Manacles and chains on tiny wrists and ankles. I stare at them stupidly, a sick feeling gnawing at the pit of my stomach. I look back over at Donovan, and I finally work out what's happening. The children are bound together in small groups, their chains staked into the ground. Donovan's pulling out the stakes, one by one, freeing the children. Another trio runs over, then another.

"Come help," Donovan shouts. "Trader, get over here!"

I take a step in his direction.

Pop-pop-pop-pop.

I freeze, see the muzzle flashes from the tree line beyond.

Pop-pop-pop-pop.

I drop to the ground. Another group of children rushes past me, their chains rattling close to my ears. They join the others behind the sandbags. Donovan ignores the incoming fire, out there in the open without any protective gear, furiously yanking up another stake. There's still half a dozen children out there with him.

"Trader!" he shouts, but my body won't move.

More children come running, green tracers flying past them. Out in the clearing, Donovan pulls up another stake, freeing more children.

It's like I'm watching it happen from outside my body, like I'm not even here. I can't feel my legs, can't hear the sound of gunfire. Everything unfolds in front of me like a silent, slow-motion movie.

Then Donovan's running in my direction, hunched over and clutching the last child to his chest.

Hurry, goddammit!

He's maybe ten feet in front of me when he's hit. His body jerks as a shot rips through his shoulder. He falls to his knees and somehow manages to set the child on the ground, who quickly scampers forward and joins the others. Donovan tries to get up, but he's hit again. His body convulses as more rounds strike him.

Then he collapses to the ground.

"GO, GO, GO!" someone shouts.

The next thing I'm aware of is boots stomping past me and into the clearing. A squad of Fundies races for the tree line, returning fire.

On hands and knees, I crawl over to Donovan. He's

lying on his side, gasping, struggling to breathe. Blood streams from the side of his mouth.

Gently, I roll him onto his back and he lets out a low, guttural groan. I lean over him, my face close to his.

"Prayer, can you hear me?"

He blinks slowly, looking at me with glassy eyes.

"I'll find a medic," I tell him. "There's gotta be a medic around here somewhere."

His breath comes in shallow, sharp inhalations. "Trader," he gasps.

"Try not to talk."

"I done horrible things in my life, Indigo…for God, for the reverend." He winces in pain, spits up blood.

I don't know what to say, what to do.

He looks at me, his eyes shining with tears. "We're more devil than angel," he sputters, "ain't we, Indigo?"

I want to answer him, to tell him something to ease his troubled mind in his final moments. But before I can say anything, his neck goes slack and his eyes fall away from me.

He's gone.

*   *   *

I'm not sure how long I sit there beside him, unaware of anything around me. Prayer Donovan's dead. The words that form that unspeakable sentence bounce around my head. It hardly seems possible. Even now, after knowing him these past days, the legend of him still looms large. So much larger than the lifeless form next to me.

You hardly knew the man, Indigo. But even as I tell myself this, I know this death, the end of this particular life, isn't one I'll forget anytime soon.

From somewhere I hear shouting, orders barked, followed by the high-pitched yelps of children. I look up, and over at the sandbags I see a pair of Fundie soldiers, chains in hand, hustling the children away.

"Stop that crying or I'll give you something to cry about!" a female soldier scolds, yanking hard on the chain in her fist, sending two children stumbling forward.

I snap out of my stupor, grabbing the shotgun next to Donovan and jumping to my feet, a sudden wave of anger coming over me. I move toward the female soldier.

In the next instant something from behind me slams into my back, sending me sprawling forward. I crash into the ground, a pair of strong arms wrapped tightly around me, a heavy body crushing the wind from my lungs. The shotgun's gone, knocked out of my hands. I try to kick, to scratch, to do anything that'll free me, but the body on top of me is too heavy, the arms too strong. A hand gets close to my mouth and I bite the hell out of it, chomping down for all I'm worth. There's a cry of pain and the hand jerks away.

Then I'm in a choke hold and in an instant I know it's over. I've choked out enough would-be suitors in my time to know I'm not getting out of this one. The hold's wrapped too tightly around my neck, locked in too deep to even move my head.

I gasp, but no air comes. "Over here, bring her over here!" someone shouts.

Next I'm off the ground, being dragged away, the arms still squeezed tight around my neck. The edges of my vision go black and I start to go out. All I can see are my legs in front of me, the heels of my boots dragging along the dirt, legs limp and useless. It's like I'm looking through a tunnel.

And then the tunnel goes dark.

CHAPTER 18

Knock, knock, knock.

Someone's at the front door. I'm too tired to drag myself up. It's not even light outside, for Christ's sake. I reach over to the other side of the bed without looking, to nudge whoever it was I brought home last night. It was that curly-haired woman, wasn't it? Jayjay, who brings those candied pecans to my turf every month, the one with the fuck-me eyes and the ass I can never resist.

But when I reach for her she's not there. I sit up in the dark, alone.

The knocking continues, then somehow it becomes a tap on my forehead.

Tap, tap, tap.

A ball of light appears. Round and orange and fuzzy around the edges.

Someone speaks. "There we go," a man's voice says. "She's waking up."

"Muy bien," a second man answers.

The ball of light shapes itself into an orange flame atop a torch pole, and the world starts to come into focus. Tall trees rise high above me. Pines. At first I can't remember where I am, then everything starts coming back: Wright and the Fundies, Donovan and Temple, the camp at Conroe with slave children. My head throbs, my hands and feet tingle.

I'm lying on my back, but not on the ground. Hands reach under me, slowly lift me into a sitting position. Everything around me lurches and spins like I've got a bad hangover. I lower my head and take a few deep breaths, trying to clear the cobwebs in my mind, to calm the nausea in my gut.

I'm sitting on a cot with two men staring down at me. One's young, his face a mask of black and green camouflage paint, his body covered with high-end battle armor. He holds an M-16 rifle and sports sidearm pistols holstered on each thigh. The other one's older and he wears no armor, only fatigues. They both have black bandannas wrapped around their heads. Black bandannas, the insignia of Guzmán's infantry troops. Neither of the two men looks particularly happy to see me.

The older one scowls, his arms folded across his barrel of a chest. He's of average height, thick-limbed with dark skin and a flat, wide nose. Southern Mexico if I had to guess his roots. Exactly the kind of face you'd expect on one of Guzmán's crew.

"So what are you," I ask, "the chief bandido?"

He rocks back in surprise, then turns to the younger soldier. "¿Y esta pendeja?"

The soldier shrugs. "You wanted a live one," he answers, "so I brought you back a live one."

The older one motions toward me angrily. "This woman look like a Fundie to you, niño?" he scolds. "You see any ink on her arms? Any crosses around her neck?"

There's a long silence as the soldier stares stupidly at my arms. The older man waits a moment for an answer, then waves his hand in disgust. "Vete ya, pinche inútil. Get the hell outta here."

"Yes, sir." The soldier slinks away, leaving me alone with the other man.

I swing my legs over the side of the cot, place my boots on the ground. My head's killing me.

"You don't look like no refugee to me, either," the man says. He squats down in front of me, eyes me carefully. "So what's your story, woman? What are you doing here?"

I rub my temples, finally noticing that the shooting's stopped. "Just a trader, compadre. Waiting for a relief mission to get here so I can do some business."

He nods, though it's the kind of gesture that says he understands what I'm saying, not that he necessarily believes it. His dark eyes are skeptical. "Here for the relief mission, huh?"

"Why else would I be here?"

"Maybe you came to see that fat preacher man," he suggests.

"Maybe that's why you came," I shoot back.

He chuckles at this. "Sure, trader."

"You're fighting for Guzmán, right? Maybe you realized you're on the wrong side and came here so the reverend could save your soul."

His grin dissolves into a snarl that on any other day would send a bolt of fear right through me. But on this night I just stare back at him, not giving a shit. I'm too worn out to care, too tired of being batted around like a ball in some kind of game.

"Watch yourself, trader," he sneers. "You ain't with friends no more. And you ain't got Prayer Donovan to protect you no more, either."

I stiffen at the mention of Donovan, my gaze falling to the ground.

"They saw you with him," the man goes on, "after he was taken down. You his woman?"

I slowly shake my head.

"What, then?" he asks. "What are you to him?"

Even if I knew the answer, I don't feel like talking to him or anyone else. Moments pass and I feel his frustration growing, his temper heating up, as he waits for me to say something.

Another soldier arrives at a jog. This one's wearing a combat helmet with night vision specs and carrying a long, slender sniper's rifle across his back.

"Sir," the soldier says, "still no sign of the target."

The man grunts. "Keep looking." The soldier gives him a yessir and leaves.

The target. Guzmán's runaway reader, surely. I wonder where she is, if she even made it out of camp.

"Come on, trader," the man exhales. "Time for you to meet the boss."

He grabs me by the elbow, stands me up. I'm woozy and my head's still pounding.

Then he lowers his chin, looks at me with a cold, serious stare. "And I wouldn't advise you to play games with him. He's not as simpático as I am."

*   *   *

Gripping my arm like a vise, he hustles me back to the center of camp. Everything's different. The shooting has stopped; so has the frantic, stampeding chaos. The only Fundies I see are dead ones, lying here and there on the ground. The tent city's quiet, eerily so.

Guzmán's soldiers really know their business. In a matter of minutes, they've taken the camp and locked it down. Don Flaco's soldiers stand guard over groups of terrified refugees. God knows what's going through their minds. For many of them, fear of Guzmán's Black Bandannas drove them here in the first place. And now, after all the hardships of traveling the open wastelands, risking everything to find a new place to live, far from that bloodthirsty madman, they find themselves smack in the middle of their worst nightmare.

The man brings me to a large tent, its canvas walls ripped with dozens of bullet tears. He pokes his head inside the door flap and mutters to someone inside.

"Adelante," a booming voice replies. Come in.

The Black Bandanna pulls me inside, and the first thing I see is Reverend Wright's desk, the same one from a couple days ago, thick and heavy with carved figures on the legs. A small battery-powered lamp sits atop it, illuminating the space with pale yellow light. Standing behind the desk, flanked by two Black Bandannas, is the man himself. Ernest "Flaco" Guzmán, in the flesh.

From the vids I've seen, I already knew he was a big man, but the small-screen images never did him justice. He's enormous, taller and thicker than even Donovan, with caramel-colored skin and a wide mustache like the Mexican revolutionaries from history books. He's wearing the same fatigues as the man at my side, and there's a sidearm on his hip. A rhino of a man, he seems to take up most of the inside of the tent.

Christ, Indigo, what a week you've had. First Wright, then Prayer Donovan, now Ernesto fucking Guzmán. From the frying pan into the fire, then into a bigger fire.

Guzmán glances at me for a moment as we enter, then turns to one of the soldiers. "¿Algo más?" he asks. Anything else?

"No, jefe," the soldier answers.

Guzmán exhales. "All right," he says, his tone disappointed. "Load up and wait for my orders. I want to be out of here in fifteen minutes."

The Black Bandanna nods. "Sí, jefe." Then he and his partner hurry past us and out the door flap.

After they leave, Guzmán picks up a pipe off the desk, then pulls a bag of tobacco out of his vest pocket. He carefully packs a large pinch of tobacco leaves into the bowl, then he looks up at the man holding my arm.

"¿Tienes cerillos?" Guzmán asks.

The man lets go of me and searches his pockets, then pulls out a box of matches and tosses it to don Flaco.

"Gracias, Chavez."

Chavez. Guzmán's right hand, his body man, a fighting

legend in his own right. I swallow, regretting every smart-ass word I uttered to him earlier.

"Who's this?" don Flaco asks, tossing the matches back to Chavez.

"A trader," Chavez answers.

Outside there's a commotion, shouting in Spanish, then three men burst through the door flap. Chavez whips out his weapon and steps protectively in front of Guzmán.

"¿Y esto, qué?" Chavez barks.

Two Black Bandannas hold a third between them, who's squirming and struggling to break free. "Let me go!" he shouts. "I didn't do nothing wrong."

Guzmán steps out from behind Chavez. "What happened?" don Flaco asks.

"We pulled him off one of the locals," the soldier on the left says.

"Una niña, maybe twelve or thirteen," adds the one on the right.

The accused soldier looks terrified. He also looks guilty as hell. Guzmán approaches them, puffs thoughtfully on his pipe. "¿Testigos?" he asks calmly, keeping his eyes fixed the accused. Witnesses?

"I pulled him off her myself, jefe," the soldier on the right tells him.

The soldier in the middle shakes his head nervously, but he's too scared to speak.

Guzmán steps forward, stares at the soldier, whose bottom lip trembles visibly. "Your jefe likes fucking more than anybody in the world, joven," don Flaco says, his voice calm and even. "But all my men know what I think about the uninvited kind. And you know it, too, don't you?"

"I won't do it again, jefe," the soldier sputters. "Se lo juro. I promise, I swear."

Without looking, Guzmán reaches behind his back, his palm facing up. As if expecting the gesture, Chavez slaps down his Beretta into don Flaco's hand. Then in one fluid, strangely graceful motion, Guzmán swings his arm forward and upward, firing off a shot just as the gun reaches the soldier's forehead. It all happens so fast, the accused barely has time to look surprised before the back of his head explodes.

The suddenness of the close-range BANG and the flare of the muzzle sends me flailing backwards into the tent wall. The next thing I know I'm on the ground, my legs still inside the tent, everything above my waist outside of it. My ears buzz with a high-pitched whine. Then a pair of hands grabs my ankles and pulls me back inside.

As Chavez helps me to my feet, the two soldiers drag the body from the tent. The dead man's face stares upward, still frozen in surprise in a way that reminds me of Valdeez. I avert my eyes from the spattering of blood and gore that covers the far wall.

I glance over at Guzmán, find him gazing at me. He's already handed the gun back to Chavez, gone back to puffing peacefully on his pipe. He studies me, then removes the pipe from his mouth.

"I'm a civilized man, you know," he states simply. "And civilized men can't tolerate barbarism."

I inhale a slow, shaky breath. *And you thought Wright was nuts, Indigo.*

He shifts his gaze to Chavez. "So this one's a trader, you say?"

Chavez nods. "Sí, jefe. She was with Prayer Donovan."

Guzmán lifts his chin when he hears the name. A sparkle lights up the warlord's eyes, and he looks at me with an interest that wasn't there a moment before.

"Bring her with us," he says.

CHAPTER 19

Minutes later, we're driving through the dark forest in a military-grade Humvee, Chavez at the wheel wearing night vision specs. I sit in the passenger side with Guzmán behind me, the only occupant of the rear seat. Don Flaco speaks into a hand radio, giving out orders with a practiced, comfortable authority that reminds me of Prayer with his squaddies. In mishmashed Spanish and English he doles out tactical instructions, telling the green group to stay close behind the yellow group. Red group, move up to take point for the next two hours.

We're surrounded by vehicles: motorbikes, trucks, Humvees, and armored buses. I can't tell how many there are since none of them have their headlights on, or any lights on for that matter, the drivers relying on night vision gear to pick their way through the thick forest of towering pines. It's like I'm traveling with an army of ghosts, the only evidence of our presence the low hum of the motors and the occasional moonlit glimpse of a nearby truck or motorboy.

It's been half an hour since we left Conroe and neither Guzmán nor his lieutenant has said a word to me. Chavez, the night specs covering the top half of his face, concentrates on the path ahead, maneuvering the Humvee around clusters of trees, keeping a slow but steady pace. I sit with my neck and shoulders tensed up, keenly aware of Guzmán's presence behind me, of the fact that he's armed and probably not in the best of moods. From his exchanges with Chavez, I gather his runaway reader, Soledad Paz—the woman he no doubt would have recovered if Donovan and I hadn't helped her out—seems to have eluded his soldiers at the Fundie camp.

Guzmán turns down the volume on his hand radio. "Trader," he says, and my heart immediately starts to race. "Tell me what you were doing back there with those Fundies."

Oh, not much, just helping the woman you're looking for escape your grasp.

My thoughts fly in a thousand directions. How much lie and how much truth do I give him? Too much of one, not enough of the other, and I'll get dumped out of this car with a bullet in my head. There's no way to know how much he already knows. He might have already twisted some Fundie arms back at camp. He may already know my whole story. I feel as if I'm being forced to walk through a minefield with a blindfold over my eyes.

I shift position, turning halfway around so I can see him. His bulk takes up most of the backseat. Moonlight coming through the window illuminates one side of his face. His gazes at me with the same calm stare he gave the rapist soldier right before he blew his brains out. I swallow, noticing the sidearm in his hand, resting casually on his knee.

Choose your words carefully, Indigo.

"They grabbed me a few days ago near my turf," I answer. "Forced me to guide Donovan's squad to Temple."

"Forced you or hired you?"

"They had my people, held them hostage till I got back."

"And where are your people now?"

"I don't know."

He nods, scratches his beard stubble. "Temple, huh? All those cars blown to mierda. We saw them when we passed through there. That was Donovan's work?"

I nod. "Yes."

"You were there?"

"Yes."

He stares at me without blinking. "You see anybody else out there in the Big Empty? Anybody besides the Unaffils?"

My mouth goes dry, my throat constricts. *Don't look away from him, Indigo. Don't break eye contact like a shitty card player.*

"No," I answer. My heart thuds against my chest.

His face is unreadable. "What about your trader channels? What's the big chatter on the shortwave right now?"

"They're talking about your fleet a lot."

"What about Temple?"

"That, too."

"Anything else?"

He's fishing. He wants to know if word's gotten out about his runaway reader.

"No," I lie.

He considers this for a long moment, during which I try to keep from pissing myself. Then finally he nods, seeming to buy my story, and it takes a real effort to keep myself from exhaling in relief. For a while neither of us speaks, and then finally I ask, "Did you get him back at Conroe? The reverend, I mean?"

Say yes, say that crazy bugger got what was coming to him.

Guzmán exhales a long, frustrated breath, then runs his hand through his hair. "The old crook got away."

"He knew we were coming," Chavez suggests sharply, breaking his long silence. "Wright ain't no pendejo. I bet he had this trader woman chained to a radio, keeping up with all the chatter. Can't tell me she didn't know nothing. When did you ever meet a trader who didn't know nothing?"

Thanks, asshole. Just when I was starting to breathe easier. Guzmán tilts his head, narrows his eyes at me. "Maybe she knew, maybe not." He shrugs. "Doesn't matter now. Spilled milk, as the gringos say."

To our right, the first light of dawn appears like a smudge of orange paint running across the horizon. We're heading north. I wonder if Guzmán knows where his runaway reader is heading. Maybe the ponytailed man gave it up, or maybe the warlord's known all along. Either way, we're rolling north in a way that seems purposeful, with a destination in mind. North toward Dallas. Heavily armed, well-protected Dallas. I wonder how far Guzmán's steel cavalry will chase after her, how close he'll dare get to the capital with its gun towers and drone patrols.

Don Flaco goes back to his radio, checking in with the black group, the purple group, the full rainbow of his fleet.

We drive on. I watch the darkness slowly give way to morning, realizing these are the first quiet moments I've had with my thoughts in what feels like a long time. Where are the greenies? Did they listen to me, or did Shooter come up with an idea he liked better? Maybe he looked at his smashed hand and had second thoughts about his future with me. I wouldn't blame him if he did.

I think about Prayer Donovan, about the children in chains, about the uselessness of everything. You work all your life, you cut smart deals, you carve out a place for yourself, but it can all go away in the blink of an eye, in the bang of a gun. *You've been such a fool, Indigo. You played the small game well, working the markets, building up your little pile of money, thinking it would protect you, thinking it would keep you safe. But you were wrong.* The big game is the *real* game, and that's the only game that truly matters. The big game's about guns and people and power. The big game's about cutting throats and taking territory and collecting scores of hardcore believers. The big game rolls right over those of us who imagine we can outsmart it, outrun it, outlast it.

Whether it's from the exhaustion of the last several hours or some unconscious need to escape my own thoughts, I find myself closing my eyelids against the blooming light of day, and I doze off. Then, what seems like only a moment later, I jerk awake to the sound of an excited voice coming out of Guzmán's radio, yammering in Spanish, saying they've spotted her, they see her. It's fully light outside now, well past dawn. For the first time I can see how many vehicles are traveling with us.

Hundreds, maybe thousands in all. More vehicles than I've ever seen in one place.

"Christ," I whisper, barely able to fathom the enormity of it. Humvees, pickup trucks, semi rigs, buses, Jeeps, motorbikes. Countless vehicles fan out for miles in all directions, organized into tight groups. Everything larger than a motorbike has some sort of mounted weapon. Grenade launchers, .50-cal machine guns, flamethrowers. A giant mob of machines and firepower, rolling over the flat, empty plains.

It has to be the warlord's entire fleet. All this for *one woman?*

Guzmán barks into the radio. "Yellow and green, you chase her down. We'll catch up. And *no shooting*, entienden? Not a single bullet or I'll have your ass."

The radio cracks with static. "Copy that, sir," someone calls back. "No shooting."

"Gordo," Guzmán barks into the radio, "you still behind me?"

"Sí, jefe," comes the answer.

"Good," don Flaco replies, then he leans forward over the seat back, his massive torso wedged between me and Chavez. He reaches across me and opens the passenger door. "I've got a pickup for you," he calls into the radio.

Chavez presses the brake and the Humvee slows, but doesn't stop. With no warning, Guzmán shoves me out of the Humvee and suddenly I'm tumbling head over ass on the ground, my arms and legs flailing. I come to a splashing stop in a sodden patch of grass. I scramble up to my feet, my face muddy and clothes soaked, as vehicles race past me like stampeding cattle. One of them, a Jeep, stops next to me and the passenger door swings open.

A man with a round body and grinning mouth full of silver teeth leans across the front seat, holding the door open.

"Buenos días, ma'am," he hollers over the noise of the passing motors. "Please get in."

*   *   *

The man called Gordo is apparently in charge of supplies, which I find out are hauled in dozens of semi trailers far behind the rest of the rolling army. According to Gordo, don Flaco must not have thought I was importante enough to keep up front with him, so he downgraded my spot in the fleet. He tells me not to take it personally. Don Flaco's a busy man.

I don't mind at all, of course. In fact, I don't even care that they tossed me into a mud puddle. Anonymity in the back of the pack suits me just fine. It feels a hell of a lot more comfortable than the hot seat of don Flaco's Humvee. "In the rear with the gear," Gordo quips, silver teeth shining. His partner, a grim-faced Black Bandanna who doesn't seem to talk at all, sits in the back.

Gordo expertly weaves the Jeep in and out of the path of the long, rectangular semis, chatting back and forth with the drivers over his radio as he makes sure their loads are secure and inspects their tires for signs of pressure loss. Then he speeds up ahead of them to find the easiest way through the countryside, sending back instructions so the large, heavy vehicles can avoid bogs or tree stumps or other obstacles. Gordo is the well-trained collie to the supply trucks' herd of sheep. After some minutes, he instructs the semis to slow down, using commands over the radio and hand signals out of his window. The fleet reduces speed, and within minutes the attack vehicles are far ahead of us, growing smaller by the moment.

Before long the supply fleet and our Jeep come to a complete stop.

"What now?" I ask.

Gordo shrugs. "We wait." He reaches down to the floorboard and retrieves a couple plastic containers.

"Breakfast, por fin," the Black Bandanna says behind me. So he does speak, after all.

Gordo passes one of the containers to his partner, then opens the other one on his lap. Tacos. My stomach rumbles at the sight of them.

Gordo looks at me, then proffers the container. "Chorizo con queso. You hungry?"

Starving. I take a couple. "Thanks." The tortillas are stale and chewy, the chorizo and cheese are cold, but I don't care. Both tacos are gone in a few bites. Gordo watches me, then hands me the container again. There's only one left. I look at him and he nods.

"Go ahead," he urges. "Food trucks'll bring me more."

Hours pass, slowly and quietly. From the backseat the Black Bandanna stays quiet, keeping an eye on me while Gordo dutifully marches up and down the long lines of supply trucks. Drivers hop down out of their cabs to confer with him. Earnest expressions and solemn nods of heads, hands in pockets. The countryside around us is flat and grassy with large clusters of oak trees, huge canopies of deep green leaves as wide as they are tall. North Texas plains. I anxiously wonder how close we are to Dallas, how close we are to the gunbird routes protecting the city. I ask the soldier in the backseat where we are, but he doesn't answer.

Time drags on and I stay rooted to the front seat. Black Bandanna won't let me leave the vehicle, doesn't even let me go take a piss in the bushes. Instead, he passes me the same cup he's been using to relieve himself all morning. In the afternoon they bring more tacos and jugs of drinking water. At dusk, Gordo returns to the Jeep and pokes his face through the driver's side window.

"Doing all right?"

"Fine," I answer. Bored as hell, but at least they haven't shot me and my clothes have dried out.

He tilts his head toward his partner. "This one talking too much for you?" He laughs at his own joke, flashing silver teeth as he grabs the Black Bandanna's shoulder and shakes it playfully. The soldier presses his lips together and furrows his brow, annoyed at Gordo's lightheartedness.

Night falls, the stars come out, and we still haven't moved. Gordo continues to make his rounds, flashlight in hand, while Mr. Talky in the backseat sits watching me silently, leaving me hours of uninterrupted time with my thoughts. Did Guzmán catch his runaway reader? The question repeats itself over and over in my head. If he has, it's bad news for this trader woman. Surely she'll talk, and when she spills the beans about the last couple days, it'll take Guzmán and Chavez about a minute to piece together that I hadn't exactly been forthright with them earlier, and that it was me and Donovan who picked up Paz in the Big Empty and later sprung her out of the camp at Conroe.

Lord, I hope you're as slippery as your guide was, Soledad Paz. If you're not, I'll be in far deeper shit than I ever was with the Fundies.

Gordo returns to the Jeep, and just as I'm about to ask him how much longer we're going to be here, there's a flash of light in the corner of my eye. I turn and look and a second flash flares, far to the north of us, lighting up the horizon with a yellow-orange glow. Someone from one of the trucks shouts, "It's started! It's started!" Then there's a cluster of flashes in quick succession, bright and then gone like a faraway lightning storm.

I watch the light show as Gordo clambers up the ladder of a semi trailer parked next to us. "¡Que se vayan a la chingada, esos ricos!" he cries as he reaches the top rung, waving his fist, followed by cheers from all around.

The explosions, too far away to hear, continue. The roof of every cab around us holds three or four people on top, watching the spectacle, cheering and shouting and waving their arms.

It finally dawns on me what's happening. Guzmán's attacking Dallas!

Christ, the man must have a death wish. Even with all those machines, with all that firepower, Guzmán's fleet is no match for the Dallasites, for their ring of fortified gun towers protecting the city and their fleet of drones raining down hell from the skies. Could he really be that crazy, that reckless?

The distant lights begin to flash brighter and more frequently as the battle heats up, a continuous succession of bursts like the high point of a fireworks show. Then, slowly over the next hour, the lag between explosions lengthens, and eventually the flashes stop altogether. The battle seems to be over.

Time passes in the darkness as I sit and wait for something to happen. Hours creep by with men and women scurrying between the semi rigs, Gordo among them, chattering into his radio, listening to the voices coming back at him. I can't make out what they're saying or what's going on. Eventually, just as dawn begins to break in the east, Gordo returns to the Jeep.

"Somebody just called for you," he announces, his silver grin tinted orange by reflected morning light.

"Who?"

"Don Flaco," he replies.

"Guzmán?"

"¡Por supuesto, trader! Don Flaco took Dallas last night!"

CHAPTER 20

There are something like three dozen gun tower compounds that form a protective ring around Dallas, spaced something like a mile or two apart. I don't know the exact numbers because I was never stupid enough to get anywhere close to one of the things. Each of them has a barracks housing who knows how many Republican Marines—zealots who love Dallas as much as Fundies love Reverend Wright—and enough firepower to take out an army. Well, most armies, I suppose, considering this latest turn of events.

So as we drive past the smoking rubble of one of these compounds, the enormity of what's apparently happened begins to hit me.

"Puta madre," Gordo says, then whistles as he surveys the destruction. "Don Flaco's boys really took it to them good."

A few Black Bandannas mill around, poking through the debris. Gordo shakes his fist triumphantly as we pass by and the soldiers return the gesture, raising their rifles overhead.

We drive on, past the tower complex, and soon the Dallas skyline comes into view. Tall, rectangular buildings, impossibly smooth and glittering in the morning sunlight. Sharp angles and perfect geometry, so unlike the crumbling, misshapen ruins of the rest of the Republic. Black smoke drifts skyward from the upper floors of some of the taller buildings.

I spot a crashed drone in a patch of tall grass ahead of us, its wings shorn off, only jagged stubs remaining, its gray body crumpled like paper and riddled with bullet holes. We drive on and I see another, this one nothing more than a smoldering tangle of metal, the landing gear poking into the air like the legs of a roasted bird.

Has Guzmán really gone and taken Dallas? It's hard to swallow, even with the evidence of it all around, lying strewn across the plains in broken, burning pieces.

The buildings grow larger and taller as we approach the city, and soon we arrive at a large camp-in-progress about a mile outside the city proper. Maybe a hundred tents dot the flat, grassy field, with more popping up every few seconds. Men and women work feverishly, pounding stakes into the ground and tying off ropes onto support poles. Gordo stops the Jeep in front of a large tent, where two Black Bandannas with M16 rifles stand guard.

"Here you go," he smiles, silver teeth gleaming.

One of the guards comes around to my side and yanks me out of the Jeep. Then he shoves me through the door flap and I stumble into the tent and the sweet smell of pipe tobacco.

"Trader!" Guzmán exclaims. "Welcome to Dallas."

He's sitting behind a simple table, the flimsy foldout kind you might play cards on, tapping the bowl of his pipe into an ashtray. On his right sits Chavez, scowling at me. And on his left sits the reader Soledad Paz.

I have to tell myself to breathe, to try to stay calm—or at least look like I'm calm—to suppress the powerful instinct to turn and run out of the tent.

Don Flaco motions to the empty chair in front of the table. "Sit."

I take a seat and Guzmán grins knowingly at me, his mustache stretching wide. "Old Chavez thought there was more to your story." He lifts his eyebrows. "And there *was* more, wasn't there? Quite a bit more."

I don't answer. Chavez glares at me, his arms folded across his chest. *Breathe, Indigo.*

Guzmán pinches a wad of tobacco from a bag on the table and refills his pipe. As he packs the bowl with his thumb, he tilts his head toward Paz. "I believe you've met Reader Soledad," he says casually. "You two are old friends from the Big Empty, I understand."

My heart sinks into my stomach. Guzmán pats his chest, searching his vest pockets for a light. Without taking his eyes off of me, Chavez places the same book of matches from yesterday on the table in front of his jefe.

"Gracias, compadre," don Flaco says, striking a flame to life, then carefully waving it over the pipe bowl. A long, tense moment passes as he sucks in a series of small puffs, lighting the tobacco and sending little plumes of smoke rising to the roof of the tent.

"Would you mind, trader," he asks, his voice cool and calm, "if I ask you a few questions?"

I clasp my hands together on my lap to keep them from trembling. "Go ahead," I answer, my mouth dry and sticky. His reader stares hard at me, studying me, her unsettling gaze steady and unblinking.

Christ, she's doing it. She's reading me!

Suddenly I'm self-conscious of everything. The tone of my voice, the position of my body, the expression on my face. *No lies, Indigo, no lies. Right now a lie gets you killed.* A small, fiendish corner of my mind laughs at the difficulty of it, at the special effort it requires. For a trader who distorts, deceives, and misdirects as naturally as breathing, speaking the truth goes against years of habit.

"Let's start with an easy one," Guzmán says with a relaxed flourish of his pipe. "What's your name?"

I take a breath. "Indigo Cruz."

He glances over at the young woman Paz. She nods.

Then he has me go over the same story I told him before, but this time in more detail. I retrace how the Fundies grabbed me and the greenies, the mission to Temple with Donovan, the unexpected discovery of his runaway reader (I include it this time), even the gruesome hours with that monster Valdeez.

Guzmán puffs on his pipe thoughtfully. "So Dealer Valdeez is out of the picture, is he?"

"Yes."

"Well done, Donovan," he mutters to himself, nodding in approval. Then he sighs and adds in a louder voice: "A great warrior, that crusader. Such a shame he fought for the wrong cause."

He presses me for information about Wright, understandably more interested in Fundie expansion strategy than my own small, unimportant story. Under the watchful gaze of his reader, I recount everything Wright said that I can remember, but it's not much, and probably not useful in the way Guzmán might like.

"He's strapped for funds," I report, rehashing what Donovan told me about the sudden death of sea trade and the cash crisis it set off.

A shark's smile spreads across Guzmán's face. "So the fat preacher's hurting, is he?"

The grin fades, though, when I tell him about Wright's debt slavery scheme to salvage his tenuous hold on his power. As I describe the children in chains, don Flaco and his reader exchange looks. The Paz woman's face reddens, a glint of anger sparking in her eyes.

Don Flaco grunts. "He's always been good with a crowd, really knows how to get them going. But he's never been good with money. Spends it as quickly as he gets it." He puffs thoughtfully, blowing a smoke ring that slowly deforms as it drifts upward. "A fool and his money, like the gringos say. You know this saying, Trader Cruz?"

"I do."

He keeps grilling me for another half hour, then he has me go over everything again. This time, though, his questions come from slightly different angles, like a jeweler examining a diamond against a bright light, looking for flaws. I give it to him straight. No omissions, no exaggerations. It's harder and more tiring than I might have imagined. The truth doesn't come nearly as easily, it turns out, as lying does. Every so often he looks over at Paz and waits for a reaction. She never says a word, only nods, which is all the confirmation Guzmán seems to need. Each time he turns to her, my insides jump around in a panic. With every nod of her head, I feel as if I've dodged a bullet.

The first time around, he didn't ask how I helped Paz escape the camp at Conroe. But now I can feel him zeroing in on it, like some kind of animal stalking prey, its predator's eyes looking for a weakness to exploit.

Then he hits me with it, hard and blunt. "So whose idea was it to spring Reader Soledad from that Fundie camp? Yours or Donovan's?"

I swallow. "Mine." The morbid thought strikes me that I may have just uttered my last word.

"But he went along with it?"

"Yes."

Guzmán takes a long, contemplative puff as he stares at me. "Interesante," he muses. "Prayer Donovan turning against Reverend Wright." Then he leans toward Chavez. "I would've bet on you crossing me before Donovan crossed the reverend."

Chavez snaps his gaze to Guzmán, surprised and clearly a bit hurt. "Jefe, jamás haría lo que ese gringo—"

"Tranquilo, compadre," don Flaco interrupts, waving his hand and chuckling to himself, amused at Chavez's discomfort. Guzmán then turns his attention back to me. "Here's the part I'm curious about, trader. You could have walked out of there clean. Your work with the Fundies was done, your people were returned to you. You could have gone home, safe and sound."

He removes the pipe from his mouth and leans forward, his eyes narrowed. "Why does a trader risk her neck for a woman she hardly knows?"

I flash to images of skin rubbed raw and bloody by iron manacles. The children's skin, my skin. I rub my wrists, the fire of my rage still burning, still undiminished after all this time. The reader Paz winces, almost imperceptibly, as if she can sense what I'm feeling, as if she's recoiling from the heat of my anger.

"I didn't want Wright to have her," I answer. "I didn't want him to use her talents." Guzmán glances over at Paz, gets a nod in return.

"And what about me?" he presses. "Do you think I should have her?" He stares at me with hawklike intensity.

Returning his gaze, I don't answer, which is as good as saying no. Maybe I've just bought myself a bullet, sentenced myself to a casual execution like the soldier rapist. Maybe I deserve it.

Guzmán regards me for a long time, his expression conveying at once curiosity and wariness, like he's not sure what to make of me, like I'm a puzzle he can't quite solve. Tobacco sizzles and cracks with each inhalation, smoke wafts upward in thoughtful puffs. Finally, the corners of his mustache curve upward in a grin.

"All right, then, trader, you're free to go."

It has to be a joke: that's my first thought. A cruel, murderous joke. As soon as I turn to leave, will he shoot me?

The reader and Chavez, as if on cue, turn toward Guzmán, their faces contorting in confusion.

"Jefe," Chavez exclaims, "we can't just let her walk away. She *lied* to us."

"So she did," Guzmán answers, standing. "But she also freed our reader. And what would have happened if she hadn't? Ask yourself that."

Chavez grunts, but doesn't answer.

Don Flaco taps the spent tobacco into the ashtray. "I'll tell you what would have happened, compadre. They would have tortured her until she gave up everything she knows about us. Then they would have forced her to work for them, to use her talents against us. Or maybe they would have cut her throat just to spite me." Guzmán looks down at me, nods appreciatively. "Trader Cruz did us a favor, getting our Soledad out of there. I can overlook a lie or two for such a favor."

Chavez frowns, looking disappointed my brains won't be decorating the wall of the tent.

My head spinning in disbelief, I nod dumbly. "I understand," I manage to say.

"Vamos, Chavez," Guzmán says, tucking his pipe into a shirt pocket. "Lots to do."

Don Flaco gives me a small nod of his head and strides out of the tent. Chavez, still scowling, follows close behind.

I look over at the reader, still trying to come to grips with the abrupt shock of my freedom. She stares back at me, her brown eyes unblinking and steady. The thought strikes me that her journey's been every bit as harrowing as mine, maybe more.

"Did you make it to Dallas before they caught up with you?" I ask, suddenly curious. My trader brain on autopilot.

A pause. "Yes."

"Why did you come here?"

"I was looking for someone."

"Did you find them?"

"I did," she sighs, her expression darkening. "But it didn't work out like I thought it would."

"Sorry," I say. Then, remembering the tank woman in Conroe, I add: "And I'm sorry for what happened to your friend."

She winces at this, and I feel bad for poking her fresh wound.

"You were a debt slave," she asks out of nowhere, "when you were a child?"

The question stuns me speechless for a moment. "How did you…?"

"It's hard to explain," she says, fidgeting self-consciously. "Sometimes I can see things."

I take a breath. "It's quite the gift you have."

She shrugs. "So they tell me."

"Well, you saw it right. I *was* a slave. Just like you are again, I guess."

Paz shakes her head. "No, it's not like that. It's not like that at all." She moves her gaze to some point beyond me. "A week ago I might have called myself that, but not now." She looks at me again, her gaze steady, a certainty in her eyes. "Now I want to be here, with Guzmán, with these people. It's where I belong."

"Then I'm glad for that," I say, a bit surprised to find that I mean it.

Paz stands. "I guess you probably want to get back to your turf now."

My turf…my turf…

"Honestly," I admit, "I'm not sure I have one to go back to."

CHAPTER 21

A Black Bandanna escorts me to a tent, telling me on the way that a car will take me back to my turf in the morning. He's a skinny kid with oversized fatigues and a pimply face.

"¿Tiene hambre, señora?"

I push my way through the door flap and settle down onto the cot. "Yeah, I could eat."

"Ahorita le mando algo." He leaves and I sit there with the flap open, watching the slow buildup of the camp, the towers of Dallas a mile behind them, dominating the landscape. A few minutes later, a white-haired woman with a deep brown face full of wrinkles brings me a hot meal of tortillas and beans.

I motion toward the bustling activity. "¿Por qué se van a acampar aquí?" Why are they making a camp here? After gently insisting that I eat something, she explains that Guzmán's people will stay here temporarily, outside the city, until the soldiers say it's safe enough for families to move in. It usually takes about a week, but with such a large city, she guesses it might take a month or more.

Later, as I'm finishing my food, the same woman returns carrying a shortwave radio with headphones and a

207

mic and sets it on the cot next to me. I stop chewing and stare at it.

"You call home," the woman suggests in hesitant, broken English. "They must be very…preocupados for you." She takes my plate and leaves.

It takes a few minutes to find the right channel, but eventually I get there. Hope's minding the shortwave today.

"Indigo!" she screeches into my headphones. "You're alive! You're alive! What happened?"

"It's a long story," I reply, still cringing from her screams.

Everyone's fine, she chirps, just fine. A wave of relief washes over me.

"Let me talk to Shooter," I sniff, choking up, my emotions surging with sudden, expected force. *Christ, Indigo, get a hold of yourself.*

"You okay, Miss Indigo?"

I wipe my eyes with my sleeve, clear my throat. "Fine. Pass me to Shooter, will you?"

"He ran over to Madisonville for supplies," she tells me.

"Madisonville?"

"You'd be amazed," she says. "He's on top of everything."

"Even with his…injury?" A sliver of shame pierces the joy of the moment.

"You know Shooter," she says. "Ain't no slowing him down."

Indeed.

She goes on, bragging on Shooter like a proud mother, recounting how he took charge as soon as they returned to home turf, how capably he's been running things since.

"Keeping the under-traders and runners busy," she crows, "making sure everything's running like clockwork. You should see him, Miss Indigo."

I sigh, giving a silent thanks to Shooter and his newly

discovered talents. Who would have ever pegged him as a competent leader?

"He's had us scanning the channels day and night since we got back," she says, "trying to find you."

I tell her I'll be back tomorrow, asking if they can manage to hold out that long on their own. She tells me not to worry. I sound tired, she says, like I need to get some rest. She insists I get a good night of sleep, nagging me until I promise I will. Hope, the mother hen.

After the call ends, I sit there for a long while. The afternoon heats up and the air inside the tent becomes stifling, so I drag the cot outside into the breeze. I watch the men and women work with quiet efficiency, setting up tents and plastic tarp shanties, hustling in and out of the supply trucks, more of which arrive constantly. It's a large operation, growing larger by the minute. People laugh and talk with excited voices as they hammer stakes into the ground and carry bundles back and forth. Children squeal and play tag, running around and under everything, the still-smoking buildings of Dallas in the near distance.

"Enrique!" a woman shouts, and I turn to look. A man wearing a black bandanna runs into the arms of a woman and they embrace each other tightly. A child, maybe four or five years old, dashes over to them, hollering Papá! Papá!, wedging himself between the couple's legs. The man kneels, removes his bandanna, and hugs the child. I think of Prayer, feeling a twinge of pain, of loss.

"You going back today?"

Soledad Paz's voice startles me. She's standing a few feet away. Washed and wearing a clean set of fatigues, she looks younger now, her smooth olive skin firm and unblemished. With her is a girl of about seven years with large round eyes, holding a tamal with both hands and making a mess of her face as she eats it.

"Tomorrow," I answer.

"You get the radio I sent over?" Paz asks.

"I did. Thanks."

Paz nods at the girl. "This is Steffa."

The kid steps behind Paz's thigh, watches me cautiously.

"I just wanted to say thanks," the reader says, stroking the girl's hair. "I didn't get a chance before."

"You're welcome."

For a long time neither of us speak, the noisy bustle around us growing louder with each passing moment.

"So what happens now?" I ask.

"I'm not sure."

Neither am I. Overnight, it seems, the world has turned upside down and inside out.

"War is coming," Paz says, echoing the same thought I've had so often lately.

I stare at the smoking buildings. "Looks like it's already here."

She turns and looks at the city. "No, this is just the beginning."

"You think so?"

She nods. "Guzmán and Wright, they have a history. Did you know?"

I shake my head.

"Not many do. Bad blood. Goes back to when they were young. Don Flaco never talks about it, but I know it's there."

I almost ask her how she knows, but then I remember who she is, what she can do. "You can *see* it?"

She nods. "He won't stop until Wright's dead."

"But he's got Dallas now," I point out. "Isn't that enough?" Seems like plenty to me.

Paz lifts her eyebrows. "If you knew him like I did, you wouldn't ask that question."

I take a moment to chew on what she's told me, on the ominous tone in her voice. If Guzmán wants to take out Wright, it won't be easy. The reverend may not be flush with cash, and he may not be holding as much turf as Guzmán, but he's still got hundreds of thousands of screaming crazies under his spell. What he lacks in tech and territory, he more than makes up for in sheer manpower. An all-out war between the two factions—if indeed that's what's coming—will be an ugly, bloody business.

"You know," she says hesitantly, "a trader with good contacts, who knows her way around the wastelands, could be a big help to us."

I look at her, confused.

She gazes at me earnestly. "We're going to need all the help we can get to take care of that preacher man."

I gape at her, stunned. "You want me to *stay* here?" I finally manage.

"Not just me," she answers, meaning Guzmán.

I shake my head, composing myself. "I have to get back to my turf, back to my life."

She nods, sighs disappointedly. "I told him that's what you'd say, but he asked me to put the offer out there anyway. He wants you to know you're welcome with us."

"Tell him thanks for me."

"I will."

Paz turns to the girl. The tamal is gone, half of it eaten, half of it stuck to her cheeks. "Lord," Paz says, playfully scolding the child, "look at you. Wipe that mess off your face, young lady."

The girl reaches up to clean her face, and that's when I notice her raw, chafed wrists.

"Was she…?" I start to ask, but the rest of the question gets stuck in my throat.

Paz nods knowingly. "In Conroe," she says. "I got her out."

Then she tousles the girl's hair. "Come on, Steffa. We need to get you cleaned up, don't we?"

We say goodbye. I watch as they walk away and disappear into the growing bustle of camp. Then I sit there for a while, watching more and more tents crop up around me, watching the children at play, running and yelling, carefree.

I start at the crackle of the radio next to me on the cot. A voice I recognize comes from the headphones. Shooter.

I cup the phones over my ears and click the microphone. "Shooter!" I cry. "I hear you're playing the big shot down there."

"Ha-ha!" he calls back. "I don't know 'bout that, Miss Indigo. Doin' what I can, I suppose."

We chat for a long while, and he catches me up with the goings-on back at the turf. He beams about the trades he made down at the market, how he haggled with that cheap one-eyed jerky vendor until he wore him out.

"Took the better part of an hour to get a good deal out of him," he tells me, his voice ringing with a trader's satisfaction.

Finally, he says: "So I guess I'll see you tomorrow, then?"

I pause, the words coming harder than I expected. "It might be a while longer than that, Trader."

"But Hope said tomorrow," he says, his voice dropping.

"I know. That's what I told her before. But there's something I have to do."

"How long's it gonna take?"

"I don't know." I force a smile into my voice. "What do you say about running things for me until I get back?"

There's a long silence in the headphones.

"Sure, Miss Indigo," he answers slowly. "I just thought you'd wanna come right away, get yourself back into the trading game."

In front of me a pack of children chase a large rubber ball, screaming and running, their bare feet tramping over the grass, the skin of their ankles and wrists smooth and unscarred.

"No, Shooter," I call back, "there's another game I have to play now."

It's a bigger game. The only game that matters.

Wish me luck, Prayer.

For free D.L. Young books, new release info, and subscriber exclusives, visit dlyoungfiction.com

ACKNOWLEDGEMENTS

First, a huge thanks to my family, who always gives me the space and quiet to write the things.

I'm also very indebted to my beta readers for *Indigo*, who were brave enough to venture into the dimly lit, frightening domain of an early draft. John Husisian (the nicest gun nut I know), Jason Kristopher (of Houston's Grey Gecko Press, buy their books!), Ira Domnitz (Esquire!), Laura Pauley Rich (for the record, my favorite feedback was the line "don't make me do this"), Veronica Smith (fellow author, look her up!), Kristin Mireles (the sweetest zombie ever), Cheryl Nelson Diariso (Chessy the Cat!), Melinda Carlson-Smith (a.k.a. Crazy Newswoman…we've known each other HOW long???), and especially Melyssa Patterson (the one, the only, I want to be like you when I grow up).

Thanks also go out to my partners in crime: Kevin, Chrissa, Chun, Cassie. You know who you are, you know what you did, and I truly appreciate it.

To my editors Juliet Ulman and Eliza Dee, my utmost thanks. If I were as good at what I do as you both are at what you do, I could quit that freaking day job.

Last, I'd like to acknowledge a few (okay, more than a few) folks I've had the pleasure to become friends with over the last few years, those who've made the ride a lot easier, and quite often loads of fun. In no particular order: Pamela Fagan Hutchins, Eric Hutchins, Bonnie Jo Stufflebeam,

William Ledbetter, Derek Künsken, Kyle Russell, Christina Rozelle, Craig DiLouie, Clane Hayward, Katie Salidas, Holly Heisey, Chris Kastensmidt, Alan J. Porter, Rebecca Thompson Nolen, Karen Rylander, Antha Adkins, Kevin Ikenberry, Hilary Ritz, Oleg Slusarenko, Shawna Stringer, Melissa Algood, Kevin Tumlinson, Rebecca Schwarz, Diane Prokop, C. Stuart Hardwick, Stina Leicht, Andi O'Connor, Michelle Muenzler, Shawn Scarber, Joy Kennedy, Holly Walrath, Elizabeth White-Olsen, Layla Al-Bedawi, Vijay Kale, Gerald Warfield, Jaye Wells, Shannon Winton, Angela Livingston, Kary English, Marianne Dyson, Martin Shoemaker, Tex Thompson, Todd Glasscock, Carrie Patel, David Boop, Ken Liu, Neil Clarke, Bill Pora, George Padgett, Austin Malone, Josh Vogt, Dusty Sabourin, John David Payne.

ABOUT THE AUTHOR

D.L. Young is a Texas-based author. He's a Pushcart Prize nominee and his stories have appeared in many publications and anthologies.

He's also the founder of the Space City Critters Writers Workshop, an English football fan, and a cigar lover.

For free books, new release updates, and exclusive previews, visit his website at www.dlyoungfiction.com.